Martyn,

Happy Birthday
and
Speedy Recovery
from

Cam

25/06/19

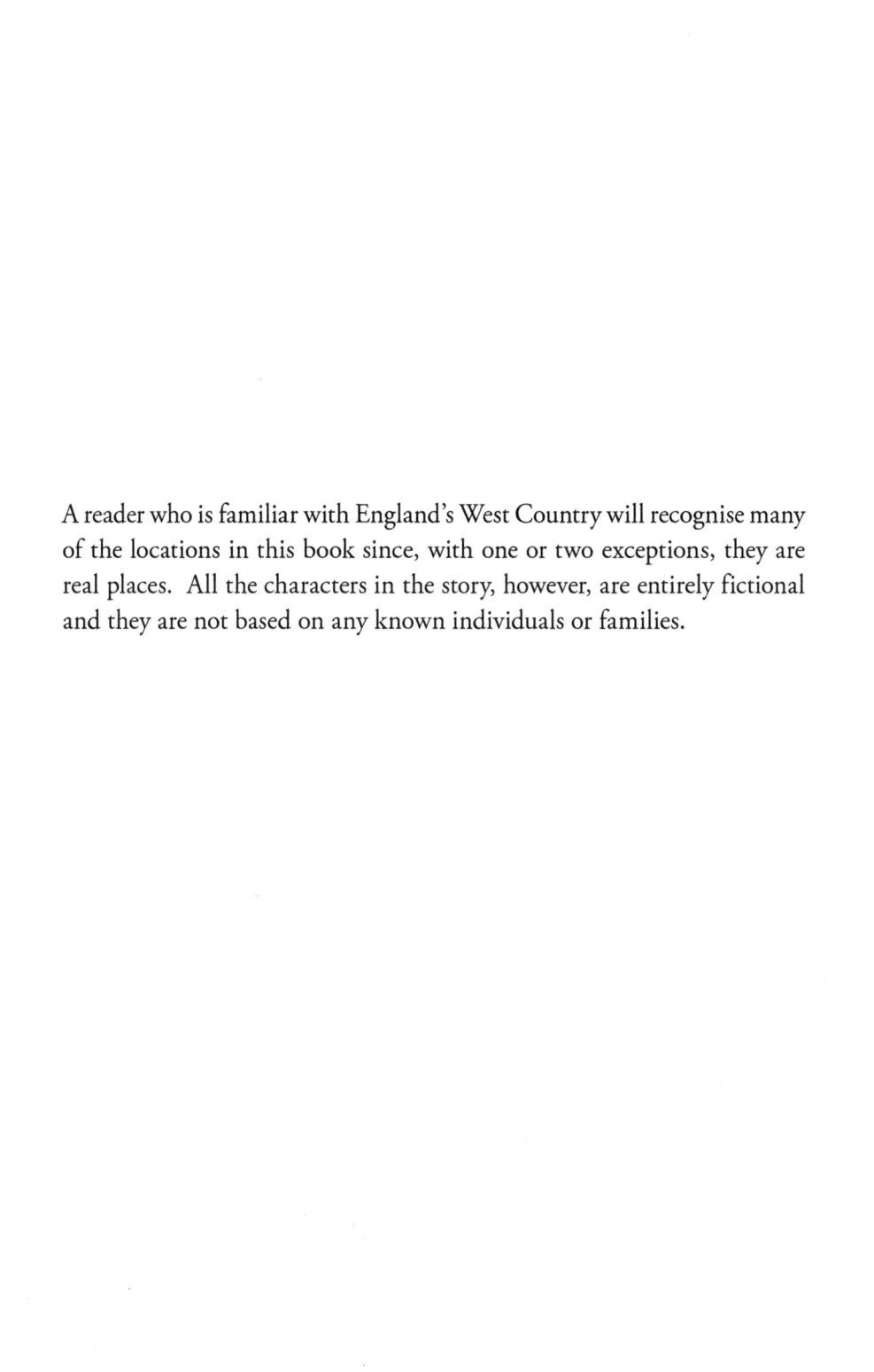

A reader who is familiar with England's West Country will recognise many of the locations in this book since, with one or two exceptions, they are real places. All the characters in the story, however, are entirely fictional and they are not based on any known individuals or families.

WESTERN WIZARDS AT *War*

Book 1: OLRIC!

CAMERON DICKIE

authorHOUSE®

AuthorHouse™ UK
1663 Liberty Drive
Bloomington, IN 47403 USA
www.authorhouse.co.uk
Phone: 0800 047 8203 (Domestic TFN)
       +44 1908 723714 (International)

© 2019 Cameron Dickie. All rights reserved.

No part of this book may be reproduced, stored in a retrieval system, or transmitted by any means without the written permission of the author.

Published by AuthorHouse 06/17/2019

ISBN: 978-1-7283-8935-6 (sc)
ISBN: 978-1-7283-8937-0 (hc)
ISBN: 978-1-7283-8936-3 (e)

Print information available on the last page.

Any people depicted in stock imagery provided by Getty Images are models, and such images are being used for illustrative purposes only.
Certain stock imagery © Getty Images.

This book is printed on acid-free paper.

Because of the dynamic nature of the Internet, any web addresses or links contained in this book may have changed since publication and may no longer be valid. The views expressed in this work are solely those of the author and do not necessarily reflect the views of the publisher, and the publisher hereby disclaims any responsibility for them.

Contents

Prologue xi

Chapter 1	Lost	1
Chapter 2	A Secret Discovery	11
Chapter 3	The First Riddle	17
Chapter 4	Polzeath	24
Chapter 5	Olric	30
Chapter 6	Theft on the train	43
Chapter 7	Lyonesse	52
Chapter 8	La Mirabelle	68
Chapter 9	Dozmary Pool	77
Chapter 10	Morgana Le Fay	88
Chapter 11	Captivity	97
Chapter 12	Despair	107
Chapter 13	The Approach to Avalon	116
Chapter 14	The Thorn Delivers	127
Chapter 15	Damsels in Distress	136
Chapter 16	The Battle of Avalon Vale	144

Epilogue 157
Afterword 161

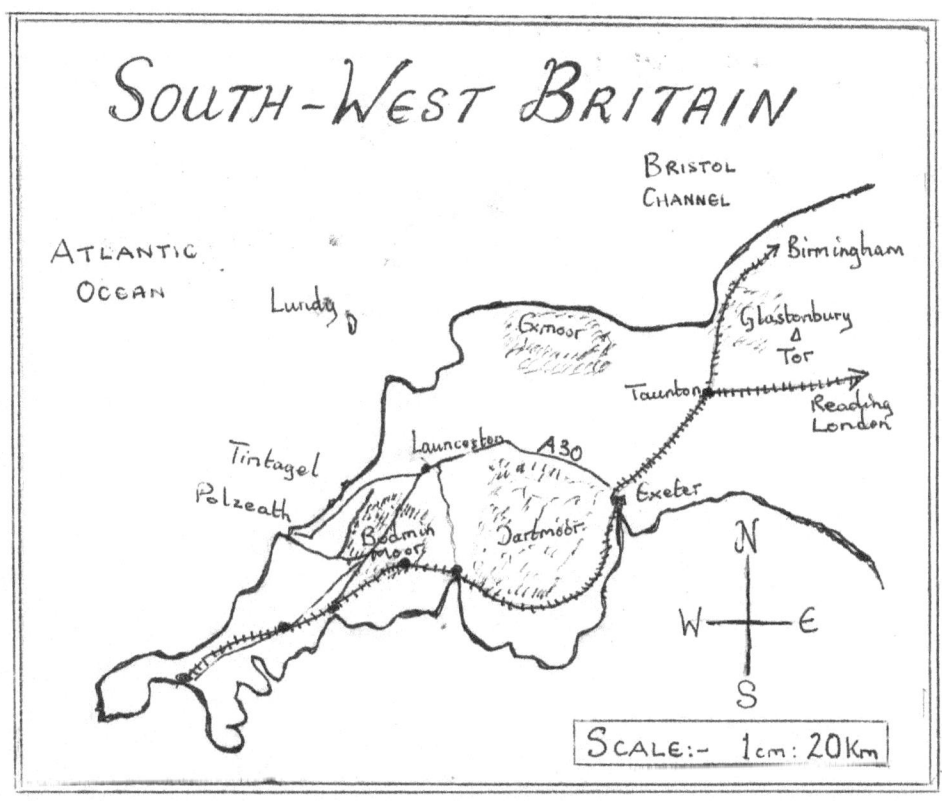

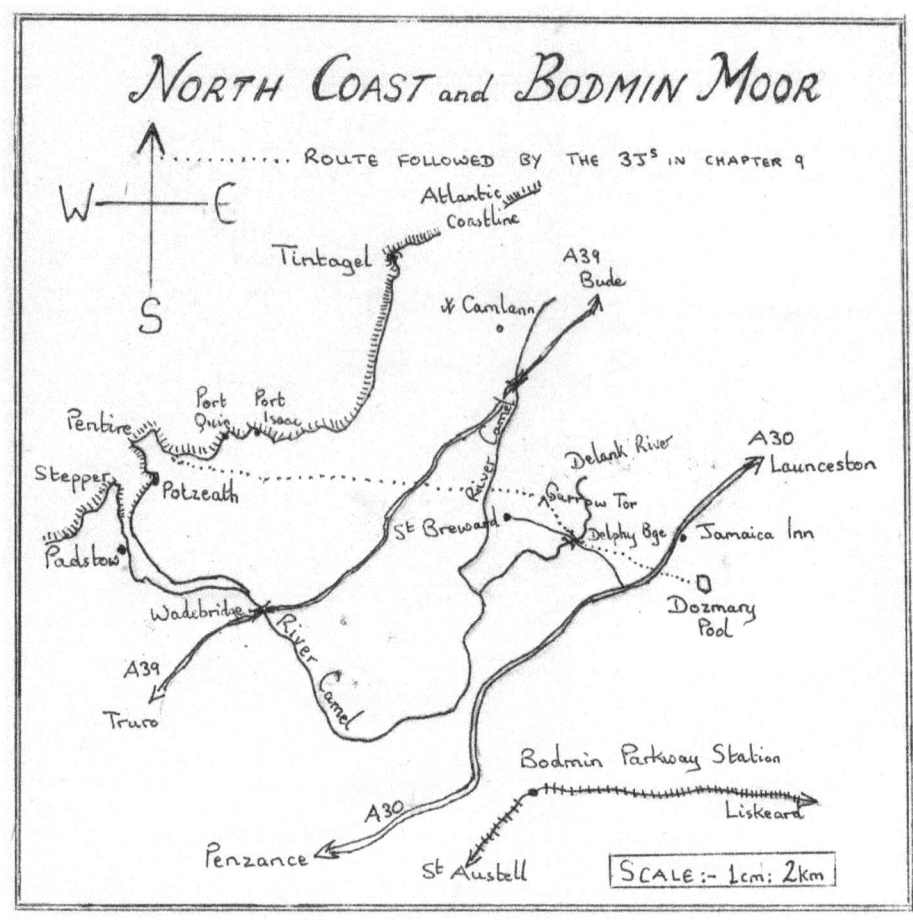

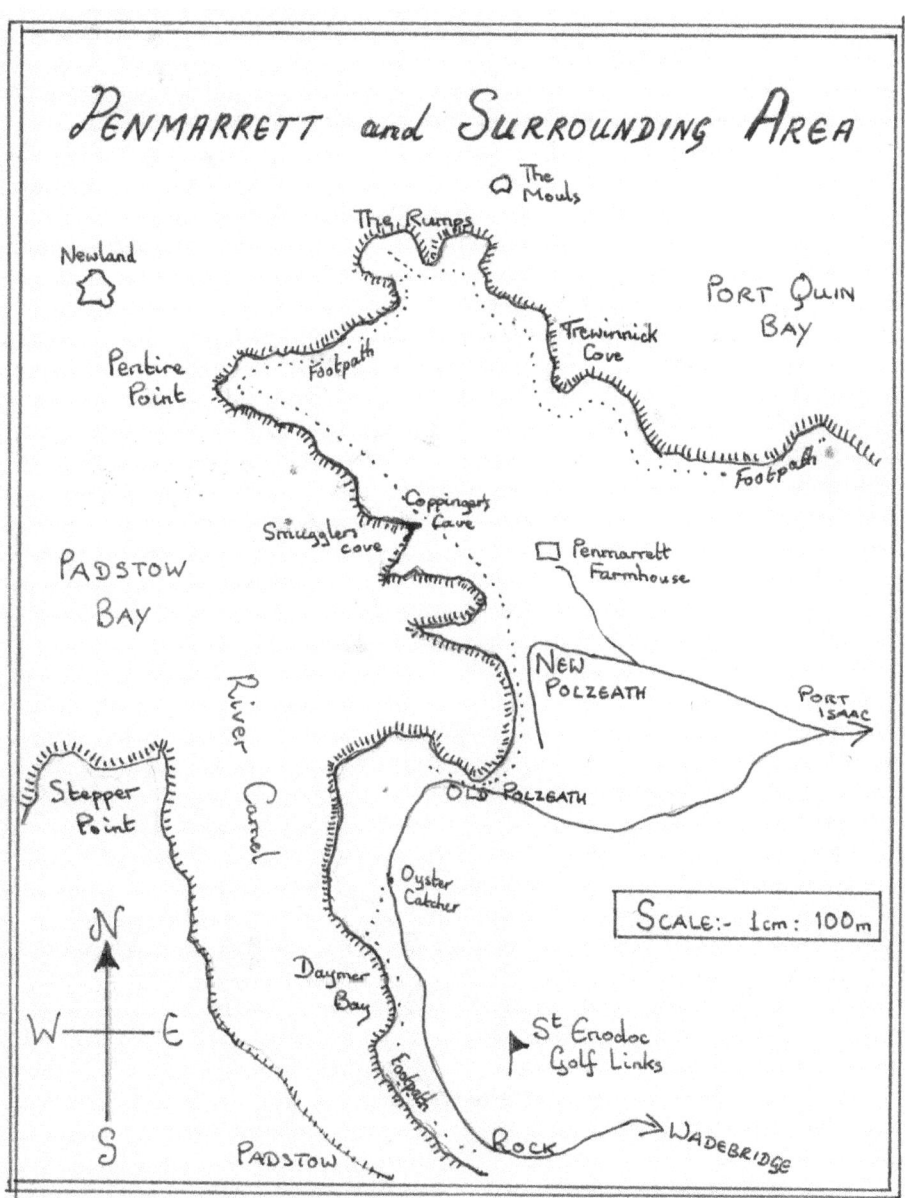

Prologue

The hot summer sun shone down on the Cornish coast, where the barley at Penmarrett Farm had been harvested earlier that day. A young field mouse scurried amongst the stubble in search of grain, unaware of the danger lurking above.

A buzzard hovered on the wing, and it would have taken only seconds to swoop down and clasp the mouse in its talons. This was an unusual buzzard. The eyes and the plumage round its neck were red. The creature served an evil cause and was ruthless, even by the standards of other birds of prey. The name of the buzzard was Olric.

The mouse was fortunate because Olric did not swoop down into the stubble but instead flew to hover over the nearby beach, invading the territory of gulls and other seabirds. Such untypical behaviour was not restricted to Olric alone. Large numbers of crows and magpies had been seen closer to the sea than normal. Ravens, often associated with bad news, had become a common sight around Polzeath.

While the field mouse continued to feed in safety, the buzzard's red eyes blazed down on a scene unfolding close to the entrance of a cave.

Chapter 1

Lost

"How about a swim?" The pages of *The Daily Express* were rustled by a loud snore, which made a sound like an elderly wild pig with indigestion. The picnic was over. Now papa was asleep, his face typically buried under the newspaper, and mama was reading her humungous holiday novel as usual. She would be occupied for hours, her big, flashy dark glasses scanning through the pages.

"Not yet. It's too soon after lunch."

The sun shone relentlessly down from the blue sky. Lola Mendes looked longingly at the sea and sighed. She was bored.

"That's nearly half an hour ago, and we didn't eat much. It was only papa who ate a pasty, and that was a jumbo one. I'm not expecting him to come too."

"Just let me finish this chapter. Then we'll go for a surf."

"Huh, that's great! We'll be having tea by then." The conversation seemed to be over, so Lola looked around for something else to do. A rubber cricket ball landed at her feet, and a large, sweaty boy in a tight wetsuit waddled over to collect it. She threw it back to him, and he murmured a sort of thank you before hurling it back in the general direction of his game. *Okay, don't ask me to play, then.* The beach seemed to be full of families playing fun games like cricket, volleyball, or tennis, and here she was alone with nothing to do. Her eyes flickered back to her parents; still no action there. *I know, I'll go and find something to do myself.*

She skipped down to the sea and paddled in the shallows, knowing how cross her mother would be. *It isn't as if I'm actually swimming,* she thought. A girl of her age surfed into the shallows before leaping back to her feet and returning into the advancing waves. Looking back at the torsos of her disinterested parents, lying some thirty metres up the beach, she wickedly hoped the cricket ball would land on papa's paper or mama's book. A little distance to her left, the rocks stretched all the way down into the sea, and she decided to see what treasures might be found on the other side. *I'll need my bucket.* She scurried back to collect it before advancing towards the rocks. Neither parent stirred.

With a furtive backwards glance, Lola stealthily climbed over the rocks. Carrying her yellow bucket, she made her way into the next bay in search of shells and pebbles and any other trophies she might find. There was no sign of anyone else in this newly discovered cove, and her mind was overcome by the loneliness of the place. It seemed so quiet here and so far from the crowds on the main beach that she felt a sense of ownership of this new uninhabited land, now revealed by the ebbing tide.

After removing her beach shoes, Lola began to explore this haven that now belonged to her, running amongst the rocks which created a natural maze on this untouched golden sand. She paused for breath and knelt down to look into a large rock pool, intrigued by the variety of creatures dwelling in their own watery world. She didn't notice a buzzard hovering high above, carefully watching her through its unusual red eyes.

She looked round, and her attention was attracted by the entrance to a cave. It resembled the mouth of an enormous whale, and she knew it just had to be explored. She jumped up and ran towards its gaping entrance. On her way, she climbed up to a ledge to check if her parents had moved. They hadn't. *They'll be so mad at me for sloping off… Oh, well. That's just too bad.* A flock of seagulls settled on a rock nearby and shrieked as if they were scolding her while she returned to her exploration. *This is exciting,* she thought. After one last look back, she nervously entered the cave.

It seemed different and less inviting than it had first appeared. It was cold and damp, yet curiosity drew her towards its hidden depths and she made her way cautiously inside. There was a steady drip of water falling from the roof, and a stale stench made her feel sick. All of a sudden, she sensed she was no longer alone, and she thought she saw movement at the back of the cave. *Maybe it's a seal. It might be injured and needing help.* She tiptoed forward. There was no seal, however, and the smell was getting worse. It was also darker and colder.

The drips were getting louder.

She began to feel scared.

Then she saw where the smell was coming from. She froze in her tracks as a huge, slimy head with one bulbous purple eye lifted and turned towards her, its vile breath enveloping her senses with its foulness. The monster made a snorting sound as it stood up, wielding what looked like an axe. Lola screamed in fear, and for a moment she was frozen to the spot. As the creature reared up to its full height, it bumped its head on the roof and snorted again. It lunged at her with its axe, and she turned to run to the warm safety of her sunny beach, where she was relieved to see another person entering the cave.

"Lola! Lola, where are you?" Her mother's anxious voice sounded a long way off, but Lola didn't care anymore about being in trouble for wandering away. She shouted back as she ran towards the daylight. The snorting was getting closer behind her, and she could sense the monster's foul smell entering her nostrils. To add to her terror, the man at the entrance to the cave had an evil look on his face. A large bird of prey hovered behind him, and its red eyes bore through her as she tried to run past him out into the open. Her scream was cut short as she was struck on the side of the head, and she knew no more as droplets of her own blood splashed over her bucket.

The buzzard hovered silently and then flew up and away over the cliff. The shrieking alarm of the gulls went unheeded on the beach, where Mr and Mrs Mendes were both desperately searching for their daughter.

"Thanks for the lift, Cyril," said Matty as he climbed out of the car.

"No problem, Matty, and good luck with your sister's kids. An 'ansom girl, your Sarah. Too good for a politician's missus, if ye do ask me." Matty Petherick waved and smiled as he closed the gate into the farmyard. He was a tall man with a ponytail of thick white hair and clear blue eyes. He walked with long strides to the back door of the house, which had belonged to his family for over four hundred years.

OLRIC!

His younger sister and her husband would be arriving that evening, and he was looking forward to spending some time with their three children during their summer holiday. Penmarrett Farm was a perfect spot for a holiday, lying close to the village of Polzeath, with its surfing beach and pretty coves, and the 3Js—James, Jo, and Jake—would make the most of every minute.

Matty removed his boots before he entered the kitchen, where he found Hilda preparing vegetables for the evening meal. "Did you find everything you needed for the spare rooms, Hilda?" he asked.

"Yes, Mr Petherick. All the beds are made, and I have left towels out." Hilda had been Matty's housekeeper for three months. Although she had proved to be extremely efficient, he found her lacking in warmth, and she didn't seem to have a sense of humour. *I wonder what Sarah and the kids will make of her? Not a great deal, I guess.* He chuckled to himself. Hilda was about forty years old with prematurely greying hair, and she had a stocky build. *I reckon she's not the sort to get on the wrong side of.* He chuckled once more, thinking of the adventurous spirit of his nephews and niece. *Fireworks in store there!*

He decided against trying to engage Hilda in any further conversation and was just about to switch on the television when he heard the sound of a helicopter passing close above his roof.

Then his mobile rang.

The powerful silver Audi moved effortlessly, weaving through the traffic on the busy A30. Soon Dartmoor would be looming on the left. Paul Briscoe felt his holiday had really begun; finally, enough miles had been placed between himself and his office at Whitehall. Whereas most MPs went abroad for their holidays, Paul preferred the peace and quiet of the West Country, and although the road was always busy, it had to be better than an airport lounge, crowded with spoilt kids, bickering parents, security checks, and likely delays.

Of course, Cornwall also tended to be crowded in the summer months, but Matty's farm would provide the peace and quiet he needed after a particularly stressful few months in government. As an added bonus, the golf course was just the place to unwind. While his family dozed and he pulled out to overtake yet another caravan, Paul contemplated the work he'd left on his desk. It would all have to wait until he returned to London, and there probably wasn't a great deal he could do in any case. Much as he would have liked to, there was little chance of his solving any of the world's crises by himself, and wherever he went, the current crisis dominating all the front pages was likely to end in disaster.

Matty listened, and his cheerful expression changed to concern. "Disappeared? ...... What? .... No trace? ...... Yes, of course, I'll be straight down. I'll take the dogs along the cliff."

Matty put his boots back on, whistled for his dogs, and walked quickly towards the cliffs. Bitzi was a young border cross collie, and he ambled playfully ahead with Jasper, an energetic black Labrador, who was a little older if not any wiser. For once, Matty did not spare them a moment's thought as he pondered the news he'd just heard: a ten-year-old girl had disappeared from the beach in broad daylight. He shuddered as his imagination ran wild, and he thought of his only niece, Jo, who was also ten. His pace quickened as he reached the clifftop leading towards Pentire Point. He peered closely over the twinkling ocean spread out before him, imagining how it might have been Jo struggling in the water as the current dragged her out to sea.

Jo stirred and looked out at the lower slopes of Dartmoor slipping past her window in a purple blur of rocks and heather. She caught sight of a horse being ridden at a gallop and was fascinated by the majestic movement of the animal and the way horse and rider seemed to be one. As they disappeared from view, Jo yearned for the chance to ride a pony of her own, like some of her friends at school, who would chat to each other about gymkhanas and pony club camps, showing off their rosettes. It wasn't so much their trophies she envied. It was the chance to care for, and share her life with, such a loyal and rewarding friend.

As it is, I've just got brothers—two of them—and that's more than enough! She glanced at them both asleep beside her. *I wonder if I could trade them both in for a pony.* At twelve, James was the eldest and definitely the most serious of the three children. He closely resembled his father in looks, with short dark hair; a round, determined jaw; and blue eyes that would dart searchingly through dark-rimmed spectacles. She giggled to herself as she imagined him addressing the House of Commons in twenty years' time, answering the awkward questions of journalists in the same belligerent way as their father did now.

She looked at her father as he concentrated on the road ahead. He indicated to overtake a line of traffic when the car in front pulled out unexpectedly, causing him to slam his foot on the brake and glance hurriedly in the mirror.

"Plonker!" he exclaimed, losing his cool.

"Really, Dad, mind your language!" To her, he was just like any other dad, although she wished he had more time to share with his family. Holidays like this didn't come around very often for the minister for defence. He worked long hours in his Whitehall office, and he always seemed to be wearing a suit. While looking at him, Jo thought how proud she was of her father, even if his responsible position kept him away from home so much.

"It's been ages since we last saw Matty." This was her mother thinking aloud as Dartmoor slid by. "Did I tell you he's got a new housekeeper? I wonder what she will make of us all."

"Yes, you did. Comes from somewhere like Romania or Poland, doesn't she? If she can cope with your brother and his eccentric ways, I should think she can put up with anything—even us lot," Paul said with a laugh. "What's her name again? You did tell me …"

"Hilda," interjected Jo excitedly. "And she'll have no problems with me. She'll be really strict with the boys, though."

"Female logic!" sighed Jake as he dug her in the ribs.

"I'm quite sure we'll all get along fine." Sarah Briscoe spoke with authority and a decisiveness that always let her family know where they stood. She was elegant and fashionable. Her blonde highlighted hair was well cut and fell neatly to just below the chin. At the moment, not a single hair was out of place. Jo smiled. *I bet it doesn't look so smart after a day on the beach!*

"Where are we, anyway?" Jo's thoughts were interrupted by her younger brother. Jake followed his mother in looks, although his fair curly hair was

Lost

as untidy as hers was immaculate. He was eight years old, and although he had a knack of irritating his sister, there was a bond between him and Jo that made them a formidable team, especially in undermining James's position as the eldest child.

"The middle of nowhere," answered Jo. "Now go back to sleep."

"I think I might. The company in the middle of nowhere isn't worth staying awake for!" retorted Jake, and his parents smiled at his reply. Jo chose to ignore this test of her wit and looked back out at the rapidly changing countryside. Like Jake, she followed her mother in looks, with hazel eyes and long fair hair that curled naturally over her shoulders. They drove on in silence, leaving the barren wastes and imposing crags of Dartmoor behind, as Paul steered the car over the River Tamar and into Cornwall.

—⚭—

Far beneath him, the main beach was alive with holidaymakers and local people scouring the shallows. The ebbing tide exposed more and more sand. Out in the bay, flotillas of small craft scurried about, and even the surfers paddled madly while trying to help in the search. Further out from the shore, Matty could see the Padstow lifeboat. The helicopter he'd seen earlier was flying at the height of the cliff, its crew looking for any sign of the missing child.

His attention was drawn to a couple standing beside a policewoman at the water's edge, their shoulders sagging with arms linked. All three were gazing out across the water, their eyes seeking a child they desperately hoped to see out amongst the waves but who simply wasn't there. *Poor people*, reflected Matty, trying to imagine the thoughts going through their minds. A crowd of bystanders seemed to be growing larger by the minute as word spread quickly along the shore.

These people are so irritating! They seemed more interested in watching the drama than helping in the search. *If they want entertainment, they may as well go back to their computer games and televisions.* He went down the steps, having to take swift evasive action to avoid being knocked over by a sturdy young man in a black leather jacket. The man seemed to be in a world of his own as he hurried to reach the top. *Some people have no manners,* thought Matty as he stepped onto the soft dry sand, making his way past litter discarded by the mindless.

With the dogs at his heels, he trod through the line of seaweed and assorted debris washed up on the high water mark, weaving a path through carefully created sandcastles. He continued onto the firmer sand which led down to the sea, passing deck chairs, towels, cricket stumps, and volleyball nets abandoned by holidaymakers. They'd all been lured across the beach to see what was going on.

The tide was quite low now, and Matty walked round the point into Smugglers' Cove, so called because of its use in past years by men such as Captain Coppinger and his band of villains. He was immediately confronted by a police officer, over whose shoulder he noticed that the area in front of Coppinger's Cave had been cordoned off with black and yellow tape. A little pair of pink and pale blue striped beach shoes lay deserted on the sand.

"I'm afraid you'll have to turn round, sir. This is a police incident zone, and members of the public are not permitted to enter." Matty turned obediently, and as he walked back towards the steps, he saw the harrowing sight of the child's parents being escorted past him towards the rocks. *Coming to identify the shoes. Poor people,* he thought. At least the crowd had been dispersed now, leaving them in some degree of privacy.

After making his way back up the steps, Matty decided to cut across Pentire and the Rumps to Trewinnick Cove. This was completely cut off from the main bay. There was a chance the child might have been carried there by the current. Whistling for his dogs, he made his way purposefully along the clifftop, thinking about Captain Coppinger and the connection between him and Matty's Petherick ancestors, but frightening visions of a helpless young girl at the mercy of the Cornish tides uppermost in his mind. When he looked down over the cove, it was as if nothing had happened where he'd just come from: *How can people just go on bathing and frolicking in the sun when such tragedy is unfolding on the other side of the headland?*

As he returned along the cliff top towards Polzeath, Matty paused once more to look down into Smuggler's Cove. He saw Sergeant Manning, the local police officer who had telephoned him earlier, accompanied by Marigold Hooper, a reporter for Radio Cornwall.

"Ah, there you are, Matty!" exclaimed the sergeant. "I believe you have met Marigold."

"Of course I have. Nice to see you, Marigold, although it would be better in happier circumstances."

"Yes, Matty, I wish I was here to ask your expert opinion on trivial parish matters or farming."

"It's the missing girl, isn't it?"

"I'm afraid so. Would you mind a short interview? It isn't just for us: it's to go out on national radio as well."

"You're welcome, Marigold, but why me? I'll do what I can to help, but there must be all sorts of other people you could interview."

"Maybe, however it's you we want. You're well-known round here, your farm runs up to the coastline, and you know more about this area than most."

"Right you are. Fire away, then."

Paul Briscoe switched on the car radio. It was five o'clock, and he could not resist the chance to listen to the news. Although he was now on holiday, he felt he had to keep up with events happening around the world. In any case, as a cabinet minister, there was every chance that he would be recalled to London if the volatile situation over global terrorism deteriorated.

At least in England there was no news of bombings or terrorist threats, but across Europe the situation was not so bright. A suicide bomber had killed thirty-six people outside the Pompidou Centre in Paris, the Playa Mayor in Madrid had been evacuated following the discovery of a suspicious package, and an outspoken critic of the Lebanese Government had been found murdered in his flat in Rome.

As thoughts moved swiftly around in Paul's mind, his wife suffered in silence. Sarah was fully aware of the gloomy political situation and she knew that Paul's duty to the country was paramount, yet she also knew how important it was for him to relax on holiday and how much his family needed to spend time with him.

Their attention was suddenly drawn by mention of Polzeath, their destination in North Cornwall, where a young girl had apparently been swept out by the tide. As this revelation sank in, the shock was compounded by the on-the-spot reporter introducing none other than "Matty Petherick, a farmer who understands tidal currents and knows the coastline like the back of his hand," to speak to the radio audience.

"Uncle Matty!" exclaimed Jo and the newly awoken Jake in unison.

"Shh," interjected James, who seemed to have woken to the BBC News as if it was an alarm clock. "Listen!"

The unmistakable tone of their uncle was already in full flow. "… And there on the sand in the middle of the cove was a pair of beach shoes. Nothing else. Just a pair of shoes." The reporter went on to ask where the tide might have taken the little girl, but Matty wasn't convinced that she had been washed out to sea. Just as he was about to elaborate, the reporter's attention switched to the chief inspector in charge of the incident, who proceeded to make an official statement.

As the car cruised farther west, the family listened in silence, and even for Paul, the political crisis faded relatively into the background as this tragedy unfolded on their holiday doorstep. The excitement at hearing Matty's voice on air had long been replaced by the knowledge that, as they drove further from doom over London, they were entering an air of gloom over Cornwall.

Chapter 2

A Secret Discovery

After breakfast, Paul and Matty went to play golf at St Enodoc while the rest of the family prepared to walk over the cliffs to spend the day on the beach. It had been a strange evening, the excitement of arrival spoilt by concerns over global and local disasters. While the adults lingered over their meal, the children had gone upstairs in the solid granite farmhouse, which had been given to the Pethericks by Queen Elizabeth I in 1589 as a reward for assisting Sir Francis Drake in defeating the Spanish Armada.

Family history was far from their minds while the three young Briscoes gazed out of the boys' open bedroom window. They watched the evening sun sink lower over the western horizon, creating dark silhouettes out of a fleet of fishing boats working offshore.

A few hours earlier, the bay had been full of vessels of all sizes, including the Padstow lifeboat, and above them two helicopters had buzzed to and fro in the search for the girl, who had now been identified as Lola Mendes, the only child of a couple from Reading. The search had been called off in the certain knowledge that no one could have survived in the sea for so long. In their different ways, all three children usually had plenty to say, but somehow none of them quite knew how to break the silence.

The first word came from an unexpected source beneath them, where Hilda had been standing on the doorstep for several minutes, unnoticed by the three children above.

"Such a tragedy, is it not?" she said in broken English. "A pretty young life lost in the sea. Children should never be permitted to wander on the

OLRIC!

shore. I hope you do not go out in those beaches." She looked up at the bedroom window. "The tides and waves are too strong for any child."

James tensed as he heard Hilda speak, for he was a proud boy who resented being treated as a child. He was about to respond when his sister, sensing his irritation, replied soothingly, "Yes, Hilda, none of us ever go near the sea alone. We don't even go near the *beach* on our own."

"That is good," was the response, and with that Hilda withdrew, shutting the door behind her.

"And good night to you too!" smarted Jo. "Don't you think she's a bit odd?"

"Not half," agreed Jake sourly, "and bossy."

"Do you think there's any chance Lola didn't go into the sea?" mused James.

"What do you mean?" asked his sister.

"I don't know. It's just something Uncle Matty said. Maybe there's some hope she's alive somewhere."

"Do you think she's been kidnapped?" suggested Jake excitedly.

"Whatever has happened must be awful, Jake, and I don't want to talk about it anymore," blurted Jo as she rushed out of the room, only to return momentarily. "And goodnight!"

Her brothers continued to stare out through the window.

"Time you went to bed, Jake. I'll be a little while," said James. His younger brother pulled a face before going to clean his teeth. Meanwhile, James continued to stare out to sea, thinking of a pair of beach shoes discovered near the entrance to Coppinger's Cave.

This new day had a freshness that helped to raise the spirits as the children and their mother made their way across the cornfields. Nearby, a buzzard hovered searching for its prey, and from a distant field came the droning sound of a combine harvester as it swept through the ripe barley, reducing the crop to stubble. Both the dogs trotted along contentedly, apparently pleased to be part of the expedition. They would probably make their own way back to the farm when they became bored with sitting on the sand.

A Secret Discovery

The tide was still coming in, and already the sea teemed with swimmers, mostly brandishing bodyboards and inflatable dinghies, as they negotiated one wave after another. Farther out where the breakers were forming, surfers in wetsuits paddled lazily about on their boards, patiently awaiting the next suitable roller that would carry them inwards towards the shallows. The lifeguards surveyed the scene from the beach, and there was a regular blast on the whistle whenever a bather drifted out of the designated area, marked by yellow flags. Following yesterday's tragedy, they were even more vigilant than usual, although no blame had been directed at them because Lola had been far away from their patrol when she had disappeared.

The family group did not go down onto the main beach, preferring the more private and secluded Trewinnick Cove, so they followed the same path Matty had trodden the previous evening. After rounding the headland and brushing through the bracken, they looked down at the smooth golden sand that they liked to consider as their own cove. Jake broke into a trot, leading the way as the family descended down the steep slope to make a base amongst the rocks enclosing the beach.

They set themselves up beside a long deep rock pool, whose bed lay obscured beneath a myriad of various seaweeds through which tiny fish and shrimps scuttled around as if playing hide-and-seek. A large red sea anemone waved prominently in the water, seeking invisible algae on which to feed. After several minutes of watching the rock pool world, James decided that the time had come for a dip in the sea, and the three children returned to base, where their mother lay soaking up the sunshine and reading her book. Having stripped down to his trunks, James started to run down across the sand, but he was brought up short by the sight of his sister placing her shoes carefully on the beach.

"I've got it!" he announced enthusiastically.

"Got what?" asked Jake, who had joined him at the water's edge.

"Come on in," called Jo, already lying in the swirling shallows. "The water's lovely."

"Feels cold to me," replied her younger brother, who hadn't waited for James's reply and who was now ankle deep. "Ow!" he yelped as he received a welcoming splash of icy water from Jo. "I'll get you!" With that, he charged towards her through the small waves.

When Jake had successfully brought down his sister, they grappled giggling in the foam. They sat up to see James still on the shore in a world of his own, looking back in the direction of the cliff.

"Let's get him," suggested Jo, and the two conspirators paddled swiftly ashore to drag him into the waves. James wasn't going to be caught, and he ran to the safety of the rocks before charging back past them to dive into an oncoming breaker.

Later, as they ate their picnic, James's thoughts returned to Jo's shoes and the way she had placed them on the sand. He decided to ask his uncle about the radio interview of the previous evening. The Briscoes were used to James's quiet meditations and thought nothing of his silence as they chatted amongst themselves and ate their pasties.

The afternoon was spent fishing in rock pools and swimming in the incoming tide. As the day wore on, they were joined by other families whose presence was mildly resented by the Briscoes, although there remained plenty of space for everyone to enjoy their holiday frolics, and Trewinnick Cove echoed to the sounds of happy voices playing in the sea, on the sand and amongst the rocks.

After a while, exhausted by their exploits, the 3Js spread themselves out on the rocks to enjoy the hot sunshine while their mother took herself into the sea. The peace was broken by Jo's indignant squeals when Jake emptied the icy contents of his bucket over her hot back. Leaping up, she chased him around the cove.

"Just wait till I catch you! You'll wish you hadn't done that, you snotty-nosed little sproglet."

It was not she, however, who brought him to a standstill. As Jake rounded a large rock at full tilt, heading towards the gaping opening to a cave, he ran straight into the bulk of a large man with a shaven head and a scar beneath his left eye.

"S-sorry," spluttered Jake, getting awkwardly to his feet.

"Got you!" yelled Jo triumphantly, grabbing him by the arm, but she didn't get her own back on her cheeky brother. The bulky stranger's presence made her feel uneasy. He said nothing as he pushed past both children, hurrying towards the path up to the top of the cliff. He stopped briefly to stare out to sea before striding out of their sight.

"Are you all right, Jake?" asked Jo, who seemed to have forgiven him.

A Secret Discovery

"Yes" he replied. "Wherever did he come from?"

"I've no idea. He was oddly dressed for the beach." Jo never failed to notice what people were wearing, which amused her brothers. However, she did have a point: a dark T-shirt, leather jacket, and jeans did look out of place on the sun-drenched beach. "He gives me the creeps," she added as she returned to join her mother by the rock pool, having completely forgotten about sorting out her younger brother.

"Did you see that man, Mum?"

"Yes, he did look a bit weird, didn't he? Fancy wearing a leather jacket on a hot day like this."

While all this went on, James was following the course of a channel like a canal connecting two pools across a wide flat rock. He was clearing the debris with a piece of slate he'd found nearby when he scooped up something unusual that was covered in slimy green seaweed. He hastened back to the higher pool to rub it clean without noticing his sister chasing his younger brother. Neither did he see a large man with a scar on his face, wearing a dark T-shirt, leather jacket, and jeans, pausing behind the rock on the other side of the pool.

It was just as well for him that the man did not see what James had in his hands.

As James eagerly scrubbed away, he saw that the object he'd discovered might have been a bell, but it was quite unlike any other bell he had come across. It was only a little bigger than his hand, was made up of many colours, and was perfectly smooth except for the handle, which was inlaid with tiny jewels. James stared at it in awe as he wondered where it had come from and how long it had been lost. It was the strangest and most beautiful thing he'd ever seen, but as he gazed at it, he found himself disappointed that it would never ring because it had no clapper. There was a bracket, but the clapper itself was gone, probably lying on the seabed or sitting as an ornament on someone's mantelpiece. While firmly clutching the soundless bell, James returned to the channel in the hope of finding the missing part or maybe some other treasure.

A tern coasted down to a nearby rock and seemed to watch him as he continued to scrape with his piece of slate. A raven perched high on the clifftop, surveying the scene below. A strong wind got up, driving a menacing dark cloud overhead, and the sea became quite rough, white horses forming angrily offshore.

"Come on, then," said Mrs Briscoe, who had just finished reading her book. "One last swim, and then we'll go back to the farmhouse." James carefully concealed the bell in his rucksack and ran towards the water to rejoin his family. If he had glanced behind him, he would have seen two magpies swoop like hawks towards the rucksack, only to find their way blocked by a flock of seabirds descending like a squadron from the sky as if to stand guard around the family's possessions.

The waves were quite strong now, crashing forcibly onto the beach, and the children had difficulty staying on their feet. After a while, they gathered in the shallows before heading back to their rock.

"Look over there!" shouted Jo excitedly, and they all looked in the direction of her outstretched arm. Their rock had been surrounded by about twenty white seabirds.

"Terns," observed her mother. "Maybe they're after the remains of our pasties." As they went back to collect their belongings, the birds took off as one and flew out to sea. The raven continued to watch the family from its vantage point as the Briscoes made their way back up through the bracken.

Later, back at the farmhouse, James decided his rucksack was not the safest place to hide his secret, so he hid the bell amongst his clothes in the chest of drawers. Unknown to him, however, he was being watched.

Chapter 3

The First Riddle

"You don't see many of those in this part of the world," observed Paul, pointing across the Camel Estuary towards Padstow, as Matty drove home from St Enodoc.

"No, it's been around here quite a lot recently. Looks way out of place amongst the fishing boats. That's for sure." The object of their conversation was a large and luxurious motor yacht which would have looked more at home in the Mediterranean than cruising off the North Cornwall coast.

"It's owned by a wealthy Frenchwoman, I gather," continued Matty. "I haven't actually met her, and she keeps herself to herself, but you do see members of her crew in the village from time to time. Peculiar lot, if you ask me."

"Anyone without a Cornish accent and the look of a pirate would seem peculiar to you, Matty," Paul noted with a laugh, "but I do agree there's something incongruous about that yacht."

"There's no need for long words either down here, Paul, and you can save your *incongruous*es for when you address Parliament."

"All right. I'm just not used to talking to Cornish farmers."

"Just remember my initials, MP, don't make me a Member of Parliament." Matty laughed, feeling quite proud of his own wit.

The two men had enjoyed their round of golf, where they had exchanged as much light-hearted banter as they were now. The Land Rover came to a halt in front of the farmhouse, and Matty got out, rather pleased with himself. He was particularly satisfied with his prowess on the fairways, where he had won the first in the series of golf matches which would continue over the coming week.

Paul clambered out, feeling a renewed sense of unease not because of defeat at golf but because Matty's witty riposte had reminded him of his duties to the nation. Up until the last minute before leaving home, he had questioned whether it was right to set off on holiday, but the prime minister himself had recommended the break would do him good. It was not, he'd been told, as if he could personally patrol all the thoroughfares of London above and below the ground, at this time of terrorist atrocities.

"Who won?" asked Jake, greeting the two men as he emerged from the house. The family had not long returned from Trewinnick Cove, and he was at a loose end.

"Shall we say your father was a very polite guest?" answered Matty. Paul smiled at this diplomatic response, and at the smirk on his younger son's face as the meaning dawned. He was sure to face a lot of teasing from his family until he turned the tables on Matty, which he was determined to do the following day.

Hilda had placed the newspapers on the hall table, and Matty picked them up as they walked through to the drawing room. The front page of the Western Express was taken up exclusively by the disappearance of Lola Mendes.

GIRL VANISHES ON CORNISH BEACH

People at the holiday resort of Polzeath have been shocked by the disappearance of a ten year old schoolgirl, who went missing in broad daylight on Saturday afternoon. Lola Mendes was spending the day on the beach with her parents when she apparently wandered into nearby Smugglers' Cove. Her beach shoes have been discovered there on the sand.

Extensive searches of the area have revealed no further clues, despite the rapid attendance of the Padstow lifeboat and two helicopters from RAF St Mawgan. A family spokesman has described Lola as 'a lively and friendly girl who enjoys life to the full'. She is about 4' 6", with dark curly hair and blue eyes. She was last seen dressed in matching yellow top and shorts.

The First Riddle

Paul was relieved that no journalists had cottoned on to the coincidence that the minister for defence was staying in the same area—a blessing for him. He silently felt guilty for his selfishness in thinking only of himself amidst such a personal human tragedy.

Matty had just disappeared into the snug to watch the news, hoping there would be some happy development in the story, when Paul's mobile vibrated with a text message. It was from the prime minister's private secretary, advising him to watch the news and contact the PM as soon as possible. Sure enough, the television screen was dominated by a glum-looking reporter, who was about to read out a highly disturbing anonymous message:

> "Island people, give way to the force
> that decrees your awful fate:
> A shooting star is set on course
> to explode in the midst of your state.
>
> When Rangoma's Comet lights the sky,
> All of Britain rests.
> The future king will surely die
> 'Midst explosions in the West.
>
> Missiles and bombs will cross the shore,
> And western power diminish.
> Britain's kingdom will be no more,
> Its relevance extinguished."

The newsreader continued to describe how this message had been received, followed by a government spokesman representing the reaction at Westminster. After this, a royal correspondent gave his account of how the news had been interpreted at Buckingham Palace. Everyone seemed to agree that this was no idle threat, and in the current political climate, it should be taken extremely seriously. Threats to members of the royal family had been made before, but in the context of global terrorism, mass destruction seemed a very real possibility, and the prospect of missiles aimed at the heart of the United Kingdom was enough to cause panic and hysteria all over the country.

Paul left the room and made a call to Chequers where, as usual, the prime minister had been spending the summer recess. He was no longer there but was making his way to Number 10, Downing Street, from where he would later address the nation. Paul had no doubt he would have to return to the capital himself, leaving Sarah and the children with Matty in the comparative safety of the North Cornwall coast.

This was a hammer blow to the Briscoes. Not only was the news shocking and worrying, but it meant the family holiday had already been spoilt when it had hardly begun. To add to their sagging spirits, there had been no developments in the Lola Mendes story, and it was now presumed certain her name had been added to the list of tragic summer drownings around the coast of Britain.

James's mind had been distracted from his thoughts of her disappearance, first by his discovery of the silent bell and then by the threat on television which had led to his father having to leave them. *I'm not going to tell anyone about the bell—not yet, anyway. There's something special and secret about it. No need to share it now.*

His thoughts, however, did drift back to footwear on the beach, and he decided to raise the subject with his uncle.

"Uncle Matty, you weren't totally convinced Lola had been swept out to sea, were you?"

"At the time no, James, I wasn't. What makes you ask?"

"When we heard you on the radio, you were about to say something when you got cut off."

"That's right. No particular reason. I think I was just trying to avoid the inevitable conclusion that she'd drowned. Also, if she had been abducted, there might still have been time to find her alive."

"Uncle, when you found the shoes on the sand …"

"Yes, go on."

"Can you remember how they were placed?"

"As it happens, yes, I can, but I don't see what you're getting at."

James felt his adrenaline begin to surge, and he really felt a sense of triumph. He wanted to make the most of his moment, so he called upstairs, hoping his sister would come down to help him.

"Jo, do you have a moment?"

"Hang on. I'll be down in a minute. I'm just looking for my fleece." After a while, she came downstairs to find her brothers waiting impatiently for her alongside Uncle Matty. "I still can't find it. I know I packed it."

"Maybe you left it somewhere," suggested Jake.

"I can't have done. I haven't worn it yet, silly! I only want it now, as it's got so cold after all that swimming."

"I'm sure it'll turn up, Jo," said Matty soothingly. "Now, let's see what your brother has been thinking about." All eyes turned towards James, who delighted in having an audience.

"Jo, could you walk towards the front door? Before you go outside, take your shoes off."

Raising her eyebrows and shrugging her shoulders, much to Jake's amusement, she did as she had been asked, placing her shoes neatly side by side on the doormat. "What about *please* take your shoes off?" she said sullenly, still tetchy about the missing fleece.

"*Please* put them on again, then," said James, calling her back and handing her shoes to her. "This time, head for the kitchen before taking them off again ... *please*." Once more, Jo did as she had been requested.

"So?" queried Jake, who had been watching the charade with puzzled amusement.

"Well, it would be no good asking you, would it?" retorted James impatiently. "You see, you don't place your shoes tidily side by side, do you? You just sling them any old where. Uncle, do you see what I'm getting at?"

"I'm afraid I must appear rather dim, James, but I don't follow you at all."

"I get it!" enthused Jo. "Is it something to do with putting them down in the direction I was heading?"

"Precisely," said James grandly. "You aren't likely to place them one way and then walk in the opposite direction, are you?" He beamed as if he had just been awarded the prize for the cleverest pupil at school. "Uncle, can you remember the direction the shoes were facing when you found them on the beach?"

"Good Lord! Yes, I can. They were placed just like Jo's, and they pointed towards the cliffs. That means Lola may not have gone into the sea when she removed her shoes. James, I do believe you may have hit on

OLRIC!

something. I must ring Sergeant Manning straightaway. There may be some hope that she hasn't drowned after all!"

"But if she didn't go in the sea …" mused Jake.

"She must have been abducted," wailed Jo. "Oh, that's just too awful. I can't bear it."

"Maybe she just got lost," said Jake. "Let's go and search for her. She could be wandering around in the cave. Come on, James."

"Oh, no, you won't!" This was Sarah Briscoe, on her way downstairs. "I am about to lose your father because he must go back to London, and who knows what awaits him there? I am not going to let my children out of my sight, and I am certainly not going to let any of you go taking risks on the shore."

Her three children remained silent. They knew that when their mother spoke so emphatically, there was never any point in trying to argue.

"Well said, Sarah. We don't want any more children being abducted. I must make that call to the police," said Matty with a finger on the side of his nose and a knowing wink to James.

"Hold on." Sarah turned to face her elder son as Matty left the room. "What on earth are you talking about? What's all this about being abducted and ringing the police?"

While Matty was in his study speaking to Sergeant Manning, the children moved through to the kitchen and told their mother about the shoes and the conclusions they had drawn with her uncle.

"Clever old James," said Jake admiringly.

Hilda stopped briefly outside the door, listening to Matty talking on the telephone. Then after entering the kitchen, she seemed to fix James with an icy stare, which made him feel slightly uneasy. Without a word, Hilda drifted through to the utility room. Her presence passed unnoticed by all except James, but he got the impression she wished their father was not the only Briscoe departing that night.

"It would be wonderful if you were right about the shoes," said Sarah, "especially with such good detective work, James. Even so, Lola's been missing for over twenty-four hours. That's a long time to have heard no news about her."

Paul had by now repacked his suitcase and was bringing it downstairs. After supper, he was going to drive back to London in order to resume his duties at Whitehall. Everyone was unusually quiet during the meal, partly because it had been a long day but mostly because of disappointment about Paul's departure and continuing worry over the fate of Lola Mendes.

The children waved as the car pulled slowly away down the lane.

"How about a walk across the fields?" suggested Uncle Matty.

"Good idea," agreed Jo.

"Do we have to? I'm tired," said Jake wearily.

"Well, you can always stay behind with Hilda," said James.

"Actually I do feel like a walk after all."

"Thought you might," his brother said, laughing.

It was a clear evening, and the sky glowed red as the sun sank over the horizon. They walked out to Pentire, looking back towards Polzeath and across the mouth of the River Camel to Stepper Point. The tide was going out, exposing more rocks and, to their right, they could look towards The Rumps.

The view reminded James about his discovery of the bell in Trewinnick Cove on the other side of the headland, and he was just wondering when to show it to the others when his uncle spoke above the sound of the breakers.

"Looks like a cracking day tomorrow," stated Matty before his attention was caught by the sight of the luxury yacht motoring eastwards a quarter of a mile offshore. This was the children's first sight of her, and he sensed their interest with amusement. She was certainly an impressive sight, cutting stylishly through the relatively calm waters out beyond the waves.

"Wow! Unreal! Look at that," exclaimed Jake.

"I wonder how many horsepower she's got?" added James, unable to resist showing off his knowledge of technical terms. "I expect she could go up to thirty knots."

James's reference to horsepower, however, reminded Jo of her yearning to ride, and of the animal she'd watched galloping on Dartmoor while they'd been travelling through Devon the day before.

As they turned to walk back to the house, no one caught sight of Hilda gazing out to sea from the clifftop away to their left. Even if they had, they still might not have noticed that she was speaking animatedly into her smartphone.

Chapter 4

Polzeath

The next day was indeed the cracker forecasted by Matty. Early morning mist gave way to a cloudless sky, and by nine o'clock, the sun was beating down relentlessly. All the papers were dominated by the anonymous threat of the previous afternoon. It had already been analysed by journalists and government, yet no one seemed to know where it had come from or what it had meant.

Were the "explosions in the west" due to occur in the west of Britain or in the western world as a whole? Was it really the heir to the English throne being targeted, or was it another future king? Could the target even be a young prince with many years ahead of him before being crowned? In spite of all suggestions and conspiracy theories, no one really seemed to have a clue.

There were also references to the "missing schoolgirl in Cornwall", and evidently some notice had been taken of James's theory that Lola had not drowned after all.

"You'd have thought they might have given me some credit," said James indignantly.

"Don't be so stuck-up, James! Remember she's still missing. You won't have anything to crow about until you actually find her yourself."

Jo's words made James feel a little ashamed, and he sulkily withdrew into a world of his own as he continued to eat his breakfast in silence.

"Where shall we go today?" wondered Jake aloud, showering Jo's plate with toast crumbs.

"Ugh! You're disgusting!" she yelled, abruptly leaving the table and flying upstairs without a further word.

Jake thought it best to keep a low profile for the time being because, for one reason or another, no one's mood quite seemed in tune with the beauty of the day.

Back in her bedroom, Jo's mood had softened, and she was on the verge of going back downstairs to join her brothers when her attention was caught by a movement outside her window. She had seen a glimpse of white feathers, and now a seabird was swooping back towards her. She stood transfixed by what she saw.

It was a tern, she thought, like those that had appeared to be guarding the family's possessions the previous afternoon. As it approached, the bird seemed to hang in the air with wings outstretched before astonishing her by landing on the windowsill. In its beak was a shiny object the size of her little finger, which she took to be a small fish. *Wow! That bird's carried that fish all the way from the sea!*

To Jo's utter amazement, the tern seemed to place the fish carefully on the windowsill before flying away back towards the cliffs. Her heart beating furiously, she opened the window out of curiosity to see if the fish was still alive. It was not, but then it never had been because it was made of metal, with eyes of rubies and scales crafted in many shades of silver. From its tail swung a hook which suggested it was an earring, but Jo decided it would serve as an excellent brooch, so she carefully attached the fish to her T-shirt with a safety pin and rushed downstairs with a renewed air of cheerfulness.

Much to her annoyance, neither of her brothers even looked up when Jo bounced back into the kitchen. She was bursting to tell them about the tern, but because neither of them had so much as noticed her reappearance, she settled down quietly at the table to finish eating her piece of toast. Out of the corner of her eye, she was relieved to see that Jake was finally coming to the end of his breakfast, and she sensed he was about to speak again.

"I hope you're not going to talk with your mouth full again, Jake!"

"Well, what do you reckon we should do today, James?"

So it's going to be like that is it? A vote taken by boys only! Jo was well able to stand up for herself, but at times like this, she did wish she had a sister to back her up.

"Better see what mum says. I'd really like to investigate the caves and see if I can find any more clues."

"We could always go down to the village and buy some sweets at the shop," suggested Jo. "We can get a postcard for dad while we're there and address it to the House of Commons. He'd be chuffed to bits!"

"That's a lovely idea, Jo," said her mother as she came into the kitchen. "He'd be thrilled to get a card from you three. Better still, a card from each of you. He'd love that." James and Jake looked at one another, raising their eyebrows. "I think we should all wander down to the village together, and maybe Uncle Matty could join us there. If you speak to him nicely, he might even buy you an ice cream."

"Let's go!" enthused Jake. "What are we waiting for?"

"The clearing up," replied his mother with a knowing smile. "No one leaves this room until it is spotless." The children groaned.

"That's all right, Mrs Briscoe. I shall see to it. I can see that the children are wishing to go, and it is such a handsome day," Hilda said. She had entered the kitchen from the back door with a basket of washing. As the children were on the verge of thanking her for the kind offer, she froze in her tracks, fixing Jo with a strange look and making the young girl feel quite uneasy for a few seconds.

"How kind, Hilda!" said Sarah. "Now, you lot, let's see if your rooms are tidy." Having already been let off the hook over the clearing up, the 3Js were so determined to make the most of the opportunity that they were halfway upstairs before their mother had finished her sentence.

"What nice children you have, Mrs Briscoe. I can see that they love being nearby to the sea."

"Yes, Hilda, they simply adore it here." As she said this, Sarah picked up a tea towel, pleased to have the chance to get to know her uncle's housekeeper a little better. "This business with the missing child, though, is a big worry when you have a young family to look after."

"Oh, I understand, Mrs Briscoe. It is so important that they do not put themselves in dangerous places, and I think it is very necessary that they do not go into the caves where they might get trapped by the tide. Also, you just do not know who you can trust when they are not in your sight."

"You are right, Hilda, and it's so sad. When I was my daughter's age, no one worried about a young girl alone in the village. I used to roam for hours on my own around this farm, and nobody gave it a moment's thought."

"Mrs Briscoe, please do not misunderstand, but I wonder if I might help you. I would be pleased to take your children down to the village, and then you can have a little time to yourself. I am sure you need to relax, and I shall see that they do not come to any harm. It would be nice to get to know them better."

"Oh, Hilda, would you really? To be quite honest, I could do with a little time on my own."

And so it was that the three young Briscoes set off down the lane with their uncle's housekeeper while their mother withdrew into the farmhouse after waving them goodbye. James walked confidently in front while Jake merrily chattered away to Hilda, whose eyes darted warily around her. Jo strolled along at the rear, running her fingers proudly over her new brooch. As she did so, she became aware of a magpie cackling overhead and a raven appearing to be watching her from a tree beside the lane. Instinctively, she removed the brooch and put it in her pocket. It was silly, really, but she knew magpies were attracted by shiny things, and she was slightly afraid of birds in any case.

Although it was still quite early, the village was already getting busy with people bustling along the narrow street. Polzeath lay at the bottom of a steep hill, and the winding road leading to the village was already lined with cars. They were queuing for the only parking spaces on the beach.

Jo's attention was drawn by some crows perched on the top of the beach shop's slate roof. She shuddered. *Why are all those birds watching me?*

Already, several families had claimed their territories, mostly settling at the foot of the cliff. Some were placing cricket stumps, and others were marking out volleyball courts. In the foreground a red Land Rover was parked beside two bronzed Australian lifeguards carefully surveying the sea. It was a normal summer morning at Polzeath, with children's laughter and shrieking seagulls rising above the sound of the surf.

No one would have guessed a young girl had disappeared from that same beach only two days ago.

"There she is," announced Matty, and the children's eyes followed his gaze out beyond the lobster pots and drying fishing nets strewn along the harbour walls. Just emerging round Pentire, a hundred metres offshore,

OLRIC!

was the luxury yacht they'd seen the previous evening. It sliced smoothly through the swell like a knife through clotted cream. It appeared to slow down as it disappeared behind the point.

"I wish I'd brought my binoculars," muttered James.

"Don't be so nosey, James," scolded Jo, who in truth was as interested in the goings-on as her brother.

"She'll be making for Padstow," said Matty. "Shall we go up to the hill and watch from above Daymer Bay? I've got to pop into the Oystercatcher anyway."

A swift climb later, they stood outside the pub and looked across the estuary. As a dinghy lay bobbing gently beside the cruiser's hull, a crewman descended the steps and took up his position at the outboard motor. He was followed by a second man, who placed himself in the bow, standing to assist the third member to disembark. This was a woman, and even from such a distance, her elegance and beauty shone across the water. She wore a flowing long white dress and a wide-brimmed lilac hat, and as she settled into her seat in the middle of the dinghy, she might have been setting out for a picnic at Henley-on-Thames.

Instead, here she was, the very image of gentility, motoring towards the rugged Cornish coast.

The family group stood transfixed as the little boat chugged towards the shore. Even Hilda appeared impressed as she surveyed the scene with a rare smile.

By now, Jake was becoming bored. He fancied the idea of doing some exploring, and he challenged his brother and sister to a race back down the hill and across the main beach. Hilda, however, reminded him of her promise to keep them all safely together, adding that they would have to stay with her.

"That's all right," countered Matty. "I'll take responsibility for them, Hilda. They won't come to any harm, and I'm staying in the village for an hour or so. You take some time off. As for you three, just make sure you're back by the beach shop at 10.30 sharp! And don't be late!"

The children yelled their thanks as they ran out onto the sand, all thoughts of elegant ladies and motor launches dismissed from their minds. Hilda gave a forced smile and took herself off in the opposite direction. She paused to look down on the dinghy that was now close to the beach, and then she levelled her gaze out towards the launch, which was gathering speed and heading back out sea. She reached into her bag for her smartphone.

Matty watched the three youngsters with a proud smile as Jake led the race across the sand. The longer strides of his brother saw the gap close until a well-timed rugby tackle brought down Jake. Jo added her slight weight to the heap as the three siblings grappled for supremacy. Matty thought of their mother putting a brave face on how things had turned out, and of Paul doing his best to fulfil his duties to the country. As the children rose and made their way to the far end of the beach, Matty turned back towards Daymer Bay. The dinghy had been moored and left there by its crew, who were making their way towards him.

Because the tide was still fairly low, it would be easy to leave the crowded areas of beach and go round the point into Smugglers' Cove. Without any further consultation, the three young Briscoes ran past the rocks and vanished from view.

Sarah was alone. Everyone admired her for her strength and support for her husband as he wrestled with the challenges of his political career. She was also the rock on which her three children were building their lives.

Yet here she was in her brother's farmhouse, alone and inwardly in utter despair. The weight of the world's problems seemed to be pressing down on her slender shoulders, and she worried about the safety and future of her three children.

Had she known quite how unsafe they were at that moment, as they vanished round the point, she would certainly have been out of her mind with worry. As it was, Sarah would soon find plenty to fear for herself.

Chapter 5

Olric

Smugglers' Cove was deserted, and the tide had left it spotless, the wet send glistening in the morning sun. It was rockier than the main beach, so this was not a good place for surfers. As bathing here was known to be unsafe, the cove didn't appeal so much to families. It was a delight, however, for those who did come round the point at low tide, when fascinating pools were exposed amongst the maze of great boulders.

When they entered the cove, the children noticed a bird of prey swooping down onto the sand, where it seemed to be watching their approach with interest.

"That's a buzzard, I think," said James, "although the red feathers round its neck are rather unusual."

"Maybe it's a red buzzard, then," suggested Jake helpfully as it took off and rose swiftly to hover high above them.

"I've heard of a red kite, silly, but a red buzzard? I don't think so!" said James with conviction.

"Just imagine what it must be like to be a mouse or something, when a thing like that dives down to attack you," said Jo, gazing upwards. "Hey, look at all those other birds sitting on the edge of the cliff! I've never seen birds lined up like that. Scary, or what!"

"Crows, aren't they?" suggested Jake.

"Yes," confirmed his brother. "Do you know the collective noun for crows?" There was a silence as all three of them gazed up at the large collection of large menacing birds perched high on the cliff top. Neither Jake nor Jo could offer an answer, so he continued. "A murder of crows."

"Charming!" aired Jo, having another nervous look above as a solitary raven came down to perch on a large chunk of grey granite. All these birds fixed their eyes on the children, who had reached the deepest pool on the beach and were gazing into its depths. The pool was flanked by rocks, which provided homes for the large crabs lurking within, their pincers always ready to attack their prey. This was close to the spot where Lola Mendes had placed her shoes two days before.

A mysterious rustling sound distracted Sarah Briscoe from her reading. It came from a room above her. *I'd better go and investigate it,* she thought, sincerely hoping it wasn't rats. Arming herself with a broom, she quietly climbed the stairs to discover who or what was causing it.

The noise seemed to be coming from the boys' room, and she tiptoed stealthily to the door. Broom at the ready, she took a deep breath and pushed the door open. She was shocked and amazed to see two magpies, one perched on the dressing table and the other pecking busily around the floor beside James's bed. Clothes had been strewn around the room, and objects had been knocked over.

When she came in, both birds opened their beaks to give a shrill cackle before flapping their wings, causing even more destruction, and they flew noisily out through the open window to land on the barn roof across the yard. After settling there, the magpies seemed to stare back towards the house, watching the boys' bedroom window with beady eyes.

Sarah turned away and breathed a huge sigh of relief, thinking how large magpies were when one saw them at close range. She gathered her composure and was beginning to tidy up the mess when she was alerted by the sound of footsteps on the stairs.

From the depths of the cave, Loveless peered out at the three figures crouching over the rock pool. *Yes, these are definitely the ones. Soon they will be at my mercy.* He looked out beyond them, where the rocks stretched out towards the breakers. Some cormorants stood drying their wings in the distance, and beyond them on a carpet of white foam, a motor yacht could be seen heading out to sea.

He could see his accomplices, McCulloch and Growles, approaching in the distance. *Good, there is no one else in sight.* His eyes switched back to the children, still absorbed in the rock pool, and smirked in anticipation of what was to follow.

All of a sudden, the buzzard swooped, and Loveless watched triumphantly as it plummeted towards its prey. The girl screamed as the bird's talons tore into her flesh before it rose once more to its lofty position level at the clifftop. The girl was sobbing loudly and was now being shepherded towards the sanctuary of the cave by her two brothers. Beyond the group of fleeing children, McCulloch and Growles were now close behind them.

"It's all right, Jo," said James. "We're almost in the cave now. You'll be safe there." He was soon to find out how wrong he was.

"My head!" wailed Jo, clutching her fringe and looking with horror at the blood seeping through her fingers. She felt faint and frightened.

For once Jake was speechless. One moment he had been peering into the depths of the pool, watching a sizeable crab grappling with a small whelk, and the next he had been alerted by flapping wings and his sister's piercing scream. He didn't know what to say as he helped his brother to settle Jo on a rocky ledge. James started to examine the cut, which thankfully turned out to be little more than a scratch. Even so, the sudden surprise and unlikely nature of the attack had left them all in a state of shock.

"What have we here?" The guttural voice seemed to echo menacingly round the cave and drew the children's startled attention to the man towering above them. When the man spoke, his tone was far from sympathetic, and all three froze in fear.

"What have you done to upset Olric?"

James gulped and took a deep breath before answering. "Olric?" he asked. "Who on Earth's Olric?"

The stranger said nothing but looked past them to the buzzard, which was still hovering above. "That is Olric," he announced proudly.

"That bird is your pet?" queried James incredulously. "It might have taken out my sister's eye!"

Olric

"Olric never attacks without reason. Perhaps your sister has stolen something that does not belong to her."

"Stolen? I've never stolen anything in my whole life!" Jo was beginning to recover her composure, and Jake thought it wise to not challenge her over things she had "borrowed" from him in the past.

"Perhaps you have something that does not belong to you." This man was not going to give up, and he fixed them with an icy glare full of venom, making each of them tremble in fear.

"Come on," said James. "We should get back to Uncle Matty. Are you Okay now, Jo?" Jo had no chance to reply because the children were confronted by two more unpleasant-looking men. One of them was Growles, whom both Jo and Jake recognised as the stranger in the leather jacket they'd run into the day before.

"I do not think your uncle will be seeing you for some time." As he said this, Loveless pushed James across to McCulloch, and then all the children were thrown around like rag dolls by the three bulky bullies. Their screams could not be heard above the noise of the birds on the cliffs.

As the young Briscoes continued to be treated in this rough manner, they became dizzier, bewildered and terrified. From time to time, amidst the continuing baiting, one of the children would fall, only to be picked up and hurled once more across the entrance to the cave.

After a while, James and Jo lay motionless on the sand. Jake, who had put up spirited resistance, was struck on the head and flung down to join them.

The last thing he thought he saw, as he drifted into unconsciousness, was the formation of three white horses rising from the swirling surf offshore. Seated on their backs appeared to be riders in blue capes, spurring them on towards the beach. Then darkness.

—⁂—

Still armed with the broom, Sarah crept behind the door, wondering who the intruder might be, for intruder it definitely was. The tread was much too light for Matty, and if it had been the children, they would have burst noisily into the house. This was a measured tread, quietly reaching the top of the stairs, and it was now approaching the children's bedrooms. The intruder paused, and Sarah could hear a door handle being turned. *It must be Jo's room*, she thought, hoping her beating heart could not be heard. Then, assuming the visitor had gone into Jo's room, she silently sneaked out onto the landing in an attempt to reach the staircase without being seen.

She was.

Matty always enjoyed his visits to the village, where he was known and respected by all the local people. He liked to conduct his business affairs in the Oystercatcher, catching up with the news and gossip and listening to the inexhaustible supply of jokes told by Denzil Caerhays, the landlord. Today wasn't a day for joking, however, as Denzil served him a cup of coffee. "Still no news about that child. Poor little mite."

"No, it's quite dreadful, and so distressing for her poor parents. Do you know where they've been staying?"

"I believe they're being looked after by friends in Camelford. Has your sister arrived yet, Matty?"

"Yes, only her husband's already had to go back to London because of that terrorist riddle."

"Oh, yes. As if things weren't bad enough without talk of bombs and such like. I expect the children are with you too. You'll have to watch them like a hawk, Matty. We can't have any more missing children on our doorstep, can we?"

Matty nodded.

After leaving the pub a little later, Matty's eyes were drawn to the roof. A larger than usual number of crows had assembled and appeared to be watching him, and the sky above was filled with very noisy seagulls, as if they were gathering for an aerial attack. *How strange,* he thought. *The birds are unusually active this morning. I wonder what's upset them?* Just then, the elegant lady from the yacht came round the corner, and he decided to introduce himself, all thoughts of birds banished from his mind.

"Hilda!" exclaimed Sarah with astonishment. "You gave me quite a shock!" In truth she was mightily relieved to see only her brother's housekeeper emerging from Jo's room.

Hilda herself jumped in surprise. She hadn't expected to meet Sarah on the landing and she replied a little breathlessly, "So I can see, Mrs Briscoe, and I am truly sorry to have surprised you. I only came up to see if your children's rooms needed to be tidied."

"The children!" said Sarah, coming to her senses. "Where are they? You were going to stay with them." When Hilda explained that they were in Matty's care, Sarah calmed down and felt a lot better now she knew her children were safe.

"Mrs Briscoe, perhaps you would like a cup of tea?"

"Oh, yes, thank you, Hilda. I think we've both had a bit of a shock up here. I must tell you about the birds I found in the boys' bedroom."

"Birds?"

"Yes, they were making a real mess in there. A pity, really. The boys had only just tidied it up!"

"Come downstairs, Mrs Briscoe, and I shall put the kettle on."

Sarah, a lot happier now that she had met neither rats nor burglars, was pleased to put her worries behind her over a cup of tea.

James, Jo and Jake were being hauled roughly to their feet and held to face their leading attacker. High above hovered Olric, who looked hungry for further prey.

"Where is it?" demanded Loveless, staring menacingly into Jo's eyes. She blinked through her tears and looked away in terrified despair. James tried to kick him on the knee and was rewarded by having his head yanked back to neck-breaking point so that when he attempted to speak, he made no more than a strangled gurgle.

"We shall find it," continued Loveless, "so you may as well hand over the bell to me now."

"Bell? We don't have any bell," pleaded Jo through her tears.

"You may not have the bell, my lovely, but you do have a part of it, don't you?"

Before she could reply, a look of horror swept across Loveless's face as he looked over her shoulders into the distance. He let go of her abruptly and fled back into the darkness of the cave. Olric shrieked and rose higher

OLRIC!

in the sky as the sound of galloping hooves grew louder from the direction of the sea.

Each captive was released, and the children turned in time to see a sight so amazing and unexpected that it might have been a dream: galloping across the sand and jumping over the rocks were three riders on white horses. They were dressed as knights from a bygone age, robed in royal blue capes and shining silver chain mail. Each wore a white tunic emblazoned with a gold cross, and their helmets glistened in the sunlight.

In his semi consciousness, Jake had not been mistaken in thinking he had seen horses and riders taking shape beyond the breakers. On they rode towards the cave, and the villains took flight, running away over Pentire.

While two of the knights stood guard at the entrance, the third one dismounted and went over to the children. He spoke with an accent which sounded French.

"Are you three okay?"

"Guess so," mumbled James, coming slowly to his senses.

Jo put her hands to her head, feeling where the buzzard's talons had struck. "Thank you," she said. "I think they might have killed us if you hadn't scared them away. Whatever did they want with us? And why did that horrible bird attack me like that?"

"It could have blinded you, even killed you," said James.

"There must be some reason," said the knight. "Is there anything you may have done that has upset the bird?"

"Certainly not!" replied Jo.

"And what about those men?" added James. "They treated the bird like a pet, as if it was trained to attack people like that."

Jake, regaining his confidence, thought out loud. "What was all the stuff about a bell?"

"Bell?" exclaimed all three knights together

"I don't know," said Jo, "but maybe this has something to do with it." She pulled the ornate fish out of her pocket. As she did so, the knights looked at each other in surprise and started to speak rapidly to one another before she continued. "I thought it was an earring or a brooch, or something like that."

"Hey! I bet that's the missing part of the bell I found yesterday," said James.

"Bell?" asked the first and second knights together.

"Where is this bell?" added the third urgently.

"What bell?" asked his brother, and James went on to describe how he had discovered his prize whilst clearing the channel in the rocks on the other side of Pentire Point.

"Where is this bell?" repeated the third knight, his tone insistent and slightly threatening.

"Back at the house. In our room. I hid it in my rucksack."

"You never told us," said Jo indignantly.

"So? You never told us about your fish brooch thing either. Where did you find that?"

"It is of no matter now," interrupted the French knight. "However you came by these things can be discussed later. Their value is beyond measure, and you must not let anyone know about their existence. You must return and act as normally as you can. On no account must you mention what has happened here. And remember: do not talk about the bell. Is that understood?" He did not await a reply and continued as he remounted. "We must meet again at midnight when the tide is at its lowest. Bring your treasures with you to where you found the bell. You must come alone."

With that, the three horsemen pulled on their reins, turned, and cantered out of sight in the direction taken earlier by Loveless, McCulloch, and Growles. The three Briscoes watched them disappearing from view. Only a few minutes had passed since Olric's attack on Jo, yet the whole pattern of their holiday had changed in that time.

"Wow! Unreal!" exclaimed Jake. "What do you make of that?"

"Amazing!" replied Jo. "I never thought I'd be rescued by knights in shining armour."

"That man in the jacket—Leatherjacketman—what do you think his game is?" wondered Jake aloud. "He seems to be following us."

"Come on," said James after a while. "We'd better get back to Uncle Matty. We'll meet later to talk about the bell and that fish brooch. I'm not too sure about coming back here in the middle of the night."

"Why?" asked Jake.

"How do we know we can trust them? They say the bell is valuable. Why should we give it up to them? They didn't seem very friendly anyway."

"I can't believe you said that! They've just saved our lives from Leatherjacketman and his mates. What's more, have you forgotten about that beastly Olric attacking me?"

"All right, Jo. I just think we ought to talk about it. That's all, okay? Anyway, we must be getting back. Uncle Matty will go mad if we're late, and it's gone 10.30 already."

With a last shuddering look into the cave, they moved stealthily back past the rock pool, went round the point, and ran into the busy bay. After the darkness of the cave it, was nice to be back in the bright sunlight, and they were relieved to see the happy crowd of people had swollen even more than before—without a sign of the three men or nasty-looking birds on the cliff.

The only visible reminder of their recent ordeal, had they looked up, was the hovering buzzard surveying the scene a hundred feet above them.

"Ah, there you are!" exclaimed Uncle Matty as they dragged themselves wearily up past the beach shop. "I was just beginning to get worried about you, trying to think what I was going to tell your mother."

"Sorry, Uncle," mumbled James. "We lost track of time."

"So these are the children of whom you speak, Monsieur Petherick?" The soft voice belonged to the lady they had earlier seen disembarking from the yacht and who was now standing beside their uncle. "Allow me to introduce myself. I am Madame Lafayette, and I come, as you might guess, from France."

"Bonjour madame," came the reply in perfect classroom French. James even went a stage further: "Je suis enchanté de vous rencontrer."

"Très bien. I am also enchanted to meet you," Madame Lafayette beamed back at him. "What polite children you have, monsieur," she said, turning to Uncle Matty. "But not very good timekeepers. Your uncle was getting worried about you. Wherever can you have been?"

"Just round the point. We got carried away watching some crabs in the rock pools." James was pleased he had not told a complete lie, and Jake was secretly impressed by his brother's slight twisting of the truth.

"But your face, ma cherie," Madame Lafayette peered closely at Jo. "You have a nasty graze there."

"One of the crabs didn't like her," cut in Jake. This most definitely was a lie, but it had the desired effect, and there were no further questions. "Is that cruiser yours?" he continued. Uncle Matty explained that they had all watched her earlier.

"Why, yes, it is indeed. But *La Mirabelle* is not here now. My crew have all gone out to sea for some fishing this morning. I decided to spend the day in this delightful village, and quite by chance, I met your charming young uncle."

Jo giggled. She had never heard Uncle Matty described as young before, and he beamed at this compliment from the beautiful Frenchwoman.

And beautiful she was. Beneath her wide-brimmed hat, her fine, flame-red hair was tucked stylishly in a bob, with a few strands dropping to her shoulders. Her face was pale ivory, with green eyes and a mouth that curled in amusement. She wore little make-up, but a scent of sweet perfume hung around her like a gentle fresh breeze. She wore earrings of silver and on her hand a ring, where the emeralds set in diamonds matched her eyes. Her dress was of silk and flowed majestically down to her ankles. On her feet, she wore shoes of silver braid the same colour as her handbag, and in her left hand she held a dainty lime-green parasol.

"Can we go out in *La Mirabelle*?" asked Jake. "S'il vous plaît," he added quickly.

"Jake!" Jo was embarrassed by her brother's cheek.

"Certainement, mon petit. It would be a grand plaisir to take you out. But I regret that cannot be." Her manner was suddenly stern, and all the children looked crestfallen. "Unless, that is, you make me a promise." All eyes looked up into her green mocking eyes. "Promise me that you will not go playing about in rock pools and caves or on beaches when you are alone. If you do not cause concern for your uncle, then perhaps I may take you out on *La Mirabelle*."

"Oh, thank you, madame. Merci beaucoup. Of course we promise, bien sûr!" James was now in full flow of showing off his French.

At this, Madame Lafayette laughed and turned back to Matty. She expressed how nice it had been to meet him and his charming family, and how she looked forward to meeting him again soon. With that, she turned and made her way down the street with her parting words. "And remember, mes enfants, to keep away from dangerous places!"

"Wow!" exclaimed Jake. "Cool or what!"

OLRIC!

"Ice creams?" offered Matty, and they all trooped happily into the beach shop, where they sat outside writing postcards to their father, unaware of the buzzard hovering overhead and the crows silently still watching them from the roofs.

—⁂—

Upon returning to the farmhouse, they were shocked to see Sarah packing her suitcase.

"We aren't going home, are we?" asked Jo anxiously.

"No, of course not, my darling. You're not going home, but I am." Despite all protests, Sarah's mind was made up. She wanted to support Paul, but at the same time she was determined the children should spend the rest of their holiday at Polzeath. "This is the safest place for the three of you, and now I've had the chance for a good chat with Hilda, I know you will be well looked after—as long as your uncle's happy about it. Matty, are you sure that will be all right?"

"Of course! You know I wouldn't dream of allowing them to leave. They've only just got here! The main thing is that you ought to stay too. After all, you could do with a holiday yourself, Sarah." His sister, however, had made up her mind, and he realised there would be no point in pursuing the argument.

Sarah Briscoe caught the afternoon train from Bodmin Parkway. Over lunch, the children had chatted enthusiastically about their meeting with Madame Lafayette, but their mother had noticed they'd had little to say about their time on the beach. She had not prompted them either, for a small cut over Jo's eye and a few bruises here and there had only indicated they must have fallen out with each other. Now would not have been a good time for any disagreements to resurface! She had, however, told the tale of the two magpies in the boys' bedroom and of her meeting with Hilda at the top of the stairs.

Although the children had been fascinated by her account of the magpies, she had not sensed the fear gripping them. Olric's attack on Jo, the violent men in the cove, and the apparent importance of the bell had suggested to them that this was no coincidence. Magpies were well-known for their liking of shiny things, and it seemed there was a group of unpleasant people who had some control over the birds around the coast.

"It's interesting the magpies were in your room," said Jo when the children sat out in the garden that evening. "If they were looking for the bell, they must have already known that I had the silver fish in my pocket."

"That must be why the hawk went for you on the beach," mused James. He had earlier checked the bell was in the rucksack, and he had now hidden it under his clothes in the chest of drawers.

"Can I see the bell, please?" asked Jo.

Considering it was now safe to produce it, James agreed to fetch it and returned to the house. He came back a few minutes later, ashen-faced and empty-handed. "It's not there. It's gone!" he said in despair, "and our room's been ransacked."

"You said you'd hidden it," accused Jo.

"No birdy, perhaps, but some*body* obviously knew," added Jake.

"Don't try to be so clever, Jake. Can't you see how serious this might be? There's obviously something highly important about my bell, and now we've lost it."

"You mean *you've* lost it, James. If it had been me, I'd have hidden it better and made sure that no one saw me." Upon saying this, Jake rose and ran indoors.

"I *did*, Jake!" James was getting more frustrated, especially because he resented being shown up by his younger brother.

"Jake's right, James." Jo's words only added to his misery, and he hung his head in despair.

"It's a good job I had my wits about me!" said Jake, rejoining them a few moments later. From his pocket he triumphantly produced the missing bell.

The moment of triumph, however, was short-lived because no sooner had he held it up than there was a beating of wings, and the sky was darkened by a large murder of crows circling high above and cawing threateningly. Half a dozen magpies settled on the garden wall, looking menacing and making strangely aggressive noises. The three children leapt to their feet and ran to the nearest point of safety, a barn stacked with the season's hay.

Although he was relieved, James was furious: "What do you think you're playing at, Jake? You've got no business to go round snooping in my things!"

OLRIC!

"And how stupid can you be, sad case?" added his sister. "Fancy showing it to the world, when we all know it's got to be kept a secret!"

"All right, blame it all on me then! Okay, so I admit I shouldn't have brought it out in the open, but at least I had it. Do you realise if I hadn't gone looking for it, the bell would have got into someone else's hands by now?"

"What do mean?" asked Jo and James in unison.

"I saw you hiding the bell when we came back from the beach. I took it out of the drawer this morning and then left everything just as I found it. James, you said your things had been ransacked. That means someone else has been in our room since I took it, and therefore someone is pretty desperate to find it."

"But who?" wondered James.

"And why?" added Jo.

"If it isn't any of us three, that leaves Hilda and Uncle Matty."

"It couldn't be Uncle Matty, Jake, so it has to be …"

"Hilda!" They all said together.

"What about those knights? I told them I'd hidden it in my room, and we know how badly they want it," suggested James. "Mind you, they don't know where we live."

"Don't forget those birds," said Jo.

"Birds can't open drawers, Jo," James pointed out gently.

Jo was not to be put down, however. "Have you forgotten Olric? That horrid man treated the hawk as a pet, and all these birds—magpies, crows, and gulls—always seem to be watching us, don't they? It might have been those men who attacked us because they knew I had part of the bell. They could only have known if someone, or something, had told them."

"Talking birds? You're crazy!" said James. "Besides, even if any of those men had got some coded avian message about where to look in the house, they would never have got past the dogs."

"What's avian?" asked Jake, who often found his brother's use of the English language beyond him.

"It means 'relating to birds', Jake. Look, I can see what you mean, Jo, but there has to be a more logical explanation. The conundrum is … what?"

"What's 'conundrum'?" asked Jake.

Chapter 6

Theft on the train

Once on the train, Sarah Briscoe found a window seat with her back to the engine in the third carriage from the front. She pushed her suitcase into the luggage rack behind her and settled back for the journey that would take about four hours. There was plenty of space left, and she had all four seats and the table to herself.

Across the aisle, a woman with her three children were playing cards, and she thought of her own family, who had just waved her off from the platform. Beyond the family group sat a morose-looking young man with an iPod in his right ear. Opposite him, with his back to her, sat another man in a tweed jacket doing the *Daily Mail* crossword.

Just then, the carriage door slid open, and a man in his late twenties hurried in. He sat down in the seat opposite her, and Sarah smiled at him. She removed her handbag from the table and placed it carefully beside her. The young man was thickset with a shaven head, and he wore a black leather jacket with a pair of Levis, but his most distinctive feature was a two-inch scar below his left eye.

He reminded her of someone, but she could not think who it was.

As the train silently gathered speed, she looked out onto the steep wooded valleys stretching below. Her mind drifted to her childhood when she'd travelled on this line with Matty. Bodmin Moor and the north coast were wild and challenging, but these deep valleys had an eerie air about them, and she used to imagine strange creatures living there without anyone knowing.

Sarah's thoughts were interrupted by the voice of the man opposite. He was speaking softly into his mobile, but his tone was quite urgent. Whatever the young man was saying said meant nothing to her because he spoke in a foreign language, of which not one word sounded remotely familiar. He seemed to be looking at her, and she wondered fleetingly whether he might even have been talking about her.

Nonsense. It must be my imagination getting the better of me!

Nevertheless, she felt more comfortable in the knowledge there were other passengers nearby.

It had already been a long day, and Sarah began to feel drowsy. She was on the verge of dropping off when the carriage door opened once more.

"Tickets, please, all passengers who joined the train at Bodmin." The ticket inspector was a cheerful young man with a mop of sandy hair and a broad Cornish accent. He clicked Sarah's ticket and added, "So you'm be travellin' to England, me luvver?"

"Yes, I'm afraid I'm going back up country," she replied, smiling at the way the Cornish considered the River Tamar a national boundary—and that England was most definitely on the other side of it! The inspector's interest moved on to the man seated opposite before continuing his journey up the carriage. Sarah drifted off to a sleep, and she didn't hear the announcement of the train's arrival at Liskeard.

She was therefore unaware of her unfriendly companion's departure.

"So if my drawer was not safe enough, where did you hide the bell, clever clogs?" asked James.

"In the loo," answered Jake proudly.

"The loo?"

"Yup. I put it in the cistern. No one ever opens that unless there's a problem with the plumbing." Both his siblings had to admit that they were impressed; this really was an unlikely place to look. "The question is what to do now about our avian conundrum." Jake was obviously eager to put his newly learnt vocabulary to immediate use.

"Yes, we are in quite a dilemma," said James. Jake was about to interrupt, but James continued. "That means having to make a choice between two alternatives, Jake. Do we tell someone about the bell, or do we go down to the beach tonight?"

"We are stuck on the horns of a dilemma," said Paul. He was meeting secretly with the prime minister and other senior members of the cabinet at Number 10, Downing Street. "Either we admit that we are at a complete loss and invite these people to come forward and negotiate, thus handing over the initiative, or we refuse to acknowledge these threats and have to face the direst of consequences if we are wrong."

"If we take the first option, we are likely to lose face. The public will not tolerate the government showing signs of weakness," commented the home secretary.

"The second is a huge gamble, placing not just the monarchy but the whole country as the stake," said the deputy prime minister, who was also chancellor of the exchequer.

"I don't suppose we have any Intelligence on these people, do we, Paul?" asked the prime minister.

"None whatsoever. Every department is looking for sources of evidence but without any success so far."

"Our allies?" the prime minister switched his attention to the foreign secretary.

"No leads there either, Prime Minister."

"In that case, I favour the second option," said the prime minister. "Any organised terrorist movement would have been identified by now. This has to be a hoax intended to cause worry and disruption to the nation. We shall ignore it. Nevertheless, all departments must remain on alert. Paul, all security forces need to be on standby, ready to be mobilised instantly if the situation demands it."

"Consider it done, Prime Minister."

"That knight on horseback told us not to tell anyone," said Jake.

"But do we know we can trust him?" asked Jo. "I mean, I know he rescued us, but who's to say he's any more honest than those nasty men in the cave? He didn't appear to be that friendly himself, and he may have only let us go because he knows we have something special. By meeting him tonight, he'll get what he wants, and then who knows what he might do with us?"

"Hang on, Jo," said James. "Back on the beach, he was 'amazing', and you went on about being rescued by a knight in shining armour. You seem to have changed your opinion of those heroes on horseback. I must admit I had my doubts at first, but somehow I think we can trust him. Obviously there's some secret about the bell, and I would like to know what it is."

"Look," countered Jo, "a girl disappears from the beach, and then we get attacked by a group of thugs in the same place. Throw in some mystery knights and a vicious crazy hawk, and you suggest we don't tell the police. Okay, I've changed my mind, but let's be realistic. If we go to the beach tonight, there may be three more disappearances—and no more clues."

Jake sided with his brother. "I vote we go. Ever since we've been down here, mysterious things have been happening around us. If we tell anyone, we'll either be laughed at or told to stay safely at home. We don't want to be treated like little kids."

"Jo, you are absolutely right, but I do feel we ought to see this through. Perhaps it would make sense to split up. Jake and I will go down to the beach at low tide, and you remain here. If we aren't back within a couple of hours, you tell Uncle Matty, and he'll know what to do."

"And what if it's already too late by then? Something dreadful might have happened to you two, and I'll take all the blame. If anyone stays behind, it should be Jake."

"Why me?"

"You're the youngest," said Jo. "I could never stay here and let my poor little brother get into danger, could I?" she teased.

"Oh, yes, leave me behind cos I'm the youngest! Just remember if it hadn't been for me, we wouldn't still have the blinking bell in any case!"

"All right," intervened James wearily. "As the Cornish say, it's one and all. In that case, we all go to Trewinnick tonight."

—ɯ—

Sarah woke up as the train crossed the Tamar and looked out over the busy estuary. Back in her youth, it had been full of naval warships, sleekly grey, lying in wait for action around the coast of Britain and in all oceans of the world. The Royal Navy had many fewer warships now, and this brought her mind back to thinking about why she was returning to London. No matter how many warships, fighter planes, and tanks, and no matter how many sailors, airmen, and soldiers were at Britain's disposal, the country could be brought to its knees by terrorists at the press of a button.

Poor Paul! What a weight of responsibility sat on the shoulders of the minister of defence and the government that he served so loyally. At least now, she would be there in a few hours' time to support him, and they could both be secure in the knowledge their children were safe in Cornwall.

The train would very soon stop at Plymouth, and no doubt it would take on a lot of passengers there, so she decided to get her book out of the suitcase before they reached the station. It would still be three hours or so before she arrived at Paddington. The family on the other side were no longer playing cards. They were all engrossed in their tablets or magazines, and none of them looked up as she moved towards the luggage rack.

Where's my suitcase?

She shakily spoke to the woman who had been playing cards. "Excuse me. My suitcase was there when I got on the train. I don't suppose you may have seen it?"

"What colour was it?" The reply came from the little boy beside her.

"Blue. Royal blue."

"Yes," the youngster piped up. "The man who was with you. I thought it was his. He got off at Liskeard. He took it."

Back at the farm, plans had been made for the evening. The 3Js had spent an hour in the barn discussing how they would sneak from their rooms and out of the farmhouse without being seen. They all loved their uncle and felt guilty to be deceiving him, but not one of them had time for Hilda, whom they considered unfriendly and disinterested in them. James reckoned she had a chip on her shoulder, which made Jake feel he would have to study her closely next time he saw her.

OLRIC!

Jo had flatly refused to be left at base camp, as she called it, whilst her brothers went on their mission. Although she still had misgivings about not seeking adult advice, she was not going to be left out of the excitement. "Besides," she had said, "the silver fish was delivered to me, wasn't it?"

That night the tide would be at its lowest at 11.50. This would mean leaving the farmhouse without disturbing the dogs at 11.15 in order to walk through the fields onto the cliffs. They would all feign tiredness after the excitements of the day. Jake would pretend to actually fall asleep after supper, and he would be steered to bed. This would prompt Jo to stay upstairs herself, and finally, James would follow suit by nine o'clock. This would give them at least two hours before they were to creep out into the Cornish darkness, and it'd still allow plenty of time for them to be there if their uncle or Hilda were to look in on them to say goodnight.

They left the barn when their plans had been made and headed across the yard to the back door of the house, which opened into the utility room. They were just going through to the kitchen when Hilda entered at the same time from the other door. This puzzled Jo because the housekeeper had departed earlier for the village, and she was sure she hadn't seen her return. From where they had been in the barn, no one could possibly have approached the house unnoticed. *We must have been concentrating even more deeply on our plans than I'd realised,* she thought.

"Did you have a nice afternoon in the village, Hilda?" asked James politely.

"Yes, thank you, very pleasant. Now I am going to prepare your tea. I think your uncle would like to eat at 6.30."

"Oh, I'll die if I have to wait that long," moaned Jake.

Sarah slumped back in her seat as the train drew into Plymouth station. She tried to remember if there had been anything of particular value in the case, and the more she thought about it, the more certain she was there was nothing worth stealing. She had already come to the conclusion that the disappearance of the case had been no accident. The man had not brought anything with him into the carriage, so it could not have been a question of his mistaking her luggage for his.

Theft on the train

Her mind was in overdrive now, and while all the remaining seats were claimed by new passengers, she pondered whether being the wife of a senior politician had made her a target. Might this theft have anything to do with the terrorist threat? Could this man work for an organisation planning to plant a bomb in the case and then have it delivered to their address? No, it was absurd. How was he to know who owned the suitcase? It had no label—that was a relief in itself—and he had boarded the train after her.

"Excuse me," said the lady across the aisle. "Aren't you going to report the theft?"

"I don't see much point now. That man could be anywhere. Besides, there wasn't anything valuable in it."

It didn't take long before the story had spread through the carriage, much to Sarah's embarrassment, especially when one passenger started to insist the authorities should be informed at once and the train searched. Fortunately, for the peace of mind of everyone on the train, a telephone call from Liskeard announced that the case had been discovered there. Sarah was quietly informed that it had been found in the gents toilet, its contents strewn throughout one of the cubicles. She had to give her name and address in case the police needed to contact her later, but fortunately no one recognised her as the wife of a senior government minister.

As the train finally pulled out of Plymouth, Sarah continued to seek some sort of explanation, but she could not think of anything a leather-jacketed, bald-headed man with a scar and a mobile phone, who didn't seem to speak English, could have been looking for in her luggage.

After tea, all the children washed up. At home, they had always had a dishwasher, and their mother had tried for years to convince her brother to introduce one to his kitchen.

"Never see the point in those things," he would say. "A wonderful time for conversation it is, washing up after a meal."

Everybody knew there was a key flaw in his argument. Uncle Matty himself had never been seen to be involved in any aspect of washing up! Nevertheless, the young Briscoes really did seem to get some enjoyment out of this old-fashioned pastime when they stayed at the farm, especially when their mother led them in a sing-song ranging from hits from the shows and traditional sea shanties to Wesleyan hymns and Cornish ballads. In Sarah's absence on this particular evening, Uncle Matty decided to act as choirmaster. This did not mean, of course, that he touched dish or cloth or water, but he was a fine singer and excelled in leading his "choir" in renditions of "Camborne Hill", "Little Eyes", and "Lamorna".

Presently, Hilda quietly left the kitchen. Jake, who did not know the words to the songs as well as the others, followed her. He had still been unable to detect the chip on her shoulder his brother had described earlier, and he thought he might be able to do so now. He was meant to be getting tired early, and if he appeared to be upset, he might attract her sympathetic attention.

> "'Twas down in Albert Square,
> And I never shall forget,
> Her eyes they shone like diamonds,
> And the evening it was wet, wet, wet,"

came the chorus from the kitchen as Hilda opened the dining room door and went inside. This room was very rarely used, although the old mahogany table was always beautifully polished. Twelve oak chairs surrounded the table, in the midst of which stood an elaborate silver candelabra. Beyond the table was a fireplace big enough to stand up in, and on each side of the fireplace was a bookcase. Apart from the huge mahogany sideboard, which dominated the wall to the right, every available space seemed to be filled with books.

> "And her hair hung down in curls,
> Her face was covered over......"

Jake had very seldom entered this room, but now he followed Hilda and was about to speak when, to his utter astonishment, he found himself alone.

"Hilda?" he called softly, but there was no response. He got down on his hands and knees and looked under the table. He inspected between the bookcases and peered around the sideboard. There was no one behind the curtains and, as he focused on the fireplace, he thought he heard a noise behind him.

She must have played a trick on him and sneaked out of the room while his back was turned. But where had she been hiding?

Jake nervously returned to the safety of the kitchen. He soon forgot about his one-sided game of hide-and-seek as he joined in with one of his favourite songs, which had a rousing and easily learnt chorus.

"Goin' up Camborne Hill, comin' down,
Goin' up Camborne Hill, comin' down,
The 'orses stood still, the wheels went around,
Goin' up Camborne Hill, comin' down."

Jake was beginning to enjoy the singing, but he didn't need reminding that he was supposed to be in need of an early night. Therefore, when Uncle Matty started to sing a heart-rending song about a tin miner losing his loved one, he yawned and announced that he was going to bed. Not very long afterwards, strictly according to plan, silence reigned upstairs while James, Jake, and Jo lay awake, their hearts pounding in anticipation as they awaited the excitement of the night ahead of them.

Chapter 7

Lyonesse

It seemed as though every floorboard creaked while they crept along the landing towards the top of the stairs. With James leading the way, they slid down the polished banisters and assembled outside the kitchen door. By now, their eyes were becoming accustomed to the darkness, although the old hallway looked rather spooky. A shaft of moonlight on the opposite wall, illuminating an aged portrait of Matty's great-grandfather, added to the spookiness.

"Let's go through the kitchen," whispered James. "The dogs will see us and won't make a fuss. If they hear the front door opening, they'll think we're burglars, which will make them bark like crazy, and we'll be rumbled before we've even started."

So it was that the 3Js passed unnoticed through the farmyard and into the fields, which led at first up a gentle slope and then down towards the sea. Away to the left, they could see some distant lights in the village, and on the right a hedge with tamarisks silhouetted against the night sky.

Ahead, the sound of the unrelenting surf drew them through the grey of the night until they stood at the top of the cliffs. Some lights were moving in the far distance—probably a freighter making its way up towards the Bristol Channel—and about half a mile offshore, some more lights indicated a fishing boat plying its trade in search of mackerel that would be on sale by breakfast time in the market at Wadebridge.

Jake's imagination came to life. His uncle had kept them all entertained for years with tales of pirates and smugglers off the Cornish coast, and of wreckers who used to lure unsuspecting sailors onto the treacherous rocks.

They would shine lights, giving the impression of providing a safe haven, and the ship's captain would realise too late he had been tricked into steering onto the rocks. As the vessel broke up and the crew was left to the mercy of the sea, the wreckers would plunder the stricken ship and steal away into the night before the coastguards arrived at the scene.

Smugglers would meet ships from France or Spain, which could not come close to the shore. They would unload the bounty of wine, brandy, and any other valuable merchandise before returning to a secluded cove, where they would conceal the spoils in a cave. A few miles down the coast, one such cave had had a secret tunnel leading to a farmhouse until the smugglers, led by Captain Coppinger, had been caught red-handed, and the cave's entrance had been blown up to prevent its use for evermore. This was a very profitable and well-organised business, but the risks involved were very high: apart from the perils of the sea, a convicted wrecker or smuggler would be hanged—the fate suffered by Coppinger—or at best deported to Botany Bay in Australia, never to return to British shores.

Jake imagined he was a coastguard, watching a boat being guided expertly by smugglers through the breakers to avoid being smashed to pieces by the half-submerged reef. He would have waited until they had slipped into the cave before summoning his men to trap them inside, catching them all red-handed.

His thoughts were interrupted by the sound of galloping hooves that could be heard above the roar of the surf.

Horses.

They were very close by, and before he had time to think, Jake felt himself being pulled to the ground by his elder brother. Jo was already lying prostrate on the springy bed of thrift, and the three of them huddled as low as they could while the galloping horses loomed fast and furious out of the darkness. On the leading animal sat a figure with long hair and a loose-fitting shirt billowing like a sail in the wind. They galloped past, the hoof beats dying into the night.

"Come on," said James, leaping to his feet. "Let's see where they went."

"We'll never catch up with them," answered Jake. "Did you see how fast they were going?"

"Yes, but they might not be going that far. We've got to go in that direction anyway."

"That's true." Whilst dreaming about smugglers and coastguards, Jake had forgotten why they had come out onto the cliffs in the first place.

Jo did not speak until they had walked round the point. "What a horseman!" she murmured in wonder. "Did you notice he was riding bareback? And he didn't even seem to have reins!"

"I wonder what they were doing," mused James. "Who on earth would be riding horses along the cliffs in the middle of the night?"

"Ponies."

"What do you mean?"

"Those weren't horses. They were ponies."

"What's the difference?" retorted her elder brother. "As far as I'm concerned, they were horses."

"Bodmin Moor ponies. They're wild, which makes that rider even more amazing."

Jo was right about these small and durable ponies, which roamed freely across the moor. They were harder to train than their cousins from Dartmoor and Exmoor, and they were therefore less commonly seen in show jumping events.

The trio reached the narrow winding path leading down through the bracken, and they descended towards the secluded beach below. They would have to make their way back round to the spot where this adventure had started some fourteen hours earlier. The new moon emerged from behind a cloud, casting eerie shadows which seemed to move silently in the breeze. Although it was a little easier to see where they were going, it was scary enough for them to huddle closer to one another as they proceeded anxiously along the path.

"So you are here after all. I was afraid that you might not come."

The children were startled and froze in their tracks, unable to see where the voice had come from. The voice was that of the Frenchman who had earlier come to their rescue. Although he sounded close, he was nowhere to be seen. A large, black-backed gull flapped its wings nearby and landed just behind a rocky outcrop ahead.

"You will follow me, if you please," continued the voice.

"We can't see you," said Jo.

"But you can if you look before you." To their astonishment, the bird fluttered back to perch on a rock, and from where it had been, there emerged the Frenchman from the shadows. "You may be surprised by many things you see this night. Not all is what it may seem, but this is neither time nor place to talk. We need to get you out of sight. You must come quickly."

There was no time for any more questions, and all they could do was follow the Frenchman down the steep slope while the bird swooped low around them. Above them, more gulls flew noisily around in circles as if waiting for breadcrumbs to be thrown to them at a picnic. At various vantage points, a lone seagull stood poised on a rock, surveying the midnight scene like a guard on sentry duty outside Buckingham Palace. James wondered if it was a strange trick of the moonlight that these birds appeared to have a faint image of a gold cross emblazoned on their breasts.

Sarah couldn't sleep. The taxi from Paddington Station had driven her through the packed streets of central London and past many of the most famous buildings in the city. As she had passed Buckingham Palace, she had noticed the flag flying on the roof indicating the presence of the monarch. The guards in their bearskins, immaculate and wary of the remotest danger, stood motionless as they protected the most important figure of the nation.

Sarah's mind reflected on the message resulting in her husband's hurried return to meet the prime minister and her own subsequent journey back to London.

Missiles and bombs will cross the shore,

And western power diminish.

Britain's kingdom will be no more,

Its relevance extinguished.

Was there any possibility these words had any connection with her stolen suitcase? If so, what did they want with her—whoever *they* were? If indeed she was a target, why didn't they take her as a hostage?

She shuddered and then remembered where she had seen the man with the scar. He had been in Trewinnick Cove the previous day, and the thought struck her that her children might be in danger after all. She tried to banish such thoughts from her imagination. The theft of her case had to be a coincidence.

OLRIC!

Finally, sleep overtook her troubled mind, and she drifted off into an uneasy slumber while, two hundred miles away, her children were descending a steep path onto a deserted beach dimly lit by the moon and buffeted by the persistent pounding of the Atlantic Ocean.

Beside her, Paul's thoughts were also in turmoil. He took the responsibility to his political party very seriously, and he had been duly rewarded for his unstinting loyalty by being honoured with such a senior post in government. More than that, however, he now felt the overwhelming burden of duty to his country as it faced its greatest threat since 1945.

The darkness seemed endless. Lying on the cold stone, it was hard to know how much space there was between the walls which enclosed the motionless body, bound in a helpless heap that had, until recently, been a lively and vibrant young girl. When she had woken up after being struck at the entrance of the cave, the tears had flown freely down her cheeks not so much from the painful thumping headache as from the bewilderment and fear of being trapped in the terrifying darkness. It was damp in this eerie cavern, and although she had been wrapped in a rug, she shivered as much through cold as the dismay and sense of loneliness gripping her.

She tried to call out, but her mouth was gagged by a tightly knotted cloth, and she was unable to untie it because her hands were bound behind her back. Her legs too were trussed together, so she was completely unable to move. She lay still in the hope of hearing a comforting sound, but apart from the distant surf, the silence was total.

Lola had no idea of time. How long had she been lying unconscious? Did anyone yet know she was missing? At first she had hoped someone would come and find her, but now the awful thought struck her that all search parties might have given up. Her parents would have been convinced to accept she had been washed out to sea. The thought of her parents made her sob once more. As the happy memories of her brief childhood echoed fleetingly around the darkened tomb, the sound of her sobbing increased. Then it ebbed to a whimper as she drifted once more into unconsciousness.

The night adventurers reached the bottom of the cliff and stepped out onto the sand in Trewinnick Cove. The Frenchman said nothing but pointed towards the sea where, in front of the incoming waves, were the ponies which had galloped past them moments before. They were standing peacefully in the shallows, looking as much at home as if they had been up on Bodmin Moor. The gulls flocked towards them, and the children felt themselves being drawn there too, all wondering how the animals had managed to cope with such a steep cliff.

"This is Dan," announced the Frenchman, introducing the horseman they'd seen earlier galloping along the cliff. "Listen to him and do whatever he says. He can be trusted." After saying this, he leaped onto the back of one of the ponies himself. Dan lifted first Jo, then Jake, and finally James onto their mounts.

"There is no need to do anything except hold on," instructed Dan in a broad Cornish accent, his eyes glinting in the moonlight. "These ponies know what to do and where they are going." His voice was gruff and slightly impatient, yet his touch was gentle and reassuring, especially for the two boys, who had never sat on a horse before.

They had no time to object because immediately they advanced like members of a cavalry regiment into the mounting surf. As they did so, the ponies seemed to be transformed into graceful white steeds, matching the colour of the foaming swell. Upon seeing the waves approaching, Jo felt exhilarated. This was like a gymkhana, and she gripped the flanks of her pony with her knees, leaning forward and low into the jump.

Up soared her pony, and it cleared the wave with ease before landing comfortably on the surface of the water and accelerating away over the incoming swell. Jo enjoyed the thrill of her ride and rose eagerly over the next wave. She looked to her right, where both her brothers appeared to be keeping up with the pace. Ahead, Dan steered a course out to sea, and the Frenchman brought up the rear, staring through the spray as it splashed around him.

They were all galloping across the sea, which was shimmering in the moonlight, and Jo could hear her brothers yelling in their nervous excitement. She joined them in the chorus while the hooves pounded along the surface of the water as if it was a sheet of rippling marble. The gulls flapped overhead, trying hard to keep up with the relentless pace being set by Dan on his white charger.

James was afraid of horses, but he had had no time for fear once he had been settled on the pony's back. Only now, when they were well offshore, did he begin to worry about where he was, realising his life depended on this pony galloping furiously across the water.

His worry turned into panic when he saw Dan's mount begin to sink gradually in front of him, and he looked down to see his own feet disappearing into the water. Jo and Jake were sinking as well, and they all started to scream while they felt themselves being drawn relentlessly into a watery grave.

Grave it may have been, but watery it was not—they remained completely dry. The sea seemed to pull back, allowing them to plough a furrow between two great rolling walls of water. Jake glanced back, his ears deafened by the roar of thundering surf, and saw the surface of the sea closing up above. This created a vast bubble of clear air through which they were still plunging headlong downwards. Stranger still was the light: they had been riding across the sea in darkness because it was still long before dawn, yet here in the gathering depths, there was a magical glow of daylight. Around them, where there had been seabirds, knights from a bygone age were floating down, their colourful cloaks acting as parachutes.

Dan began to slow down, and the ponies behind followed his lead. The bottom of the sea now loomed into view, and from the seabed there arose trees and buildings, where there might have been seaweed and rocks. Soon they could distinguish the battlements of an ancient castle, rising up in a huge rocky mass overshadowing the houses which stood around it. Banners flew from the turrets, and from the centre tower fluttered a flag showing a gold cross on a background of the deepest crimson. Beneath the cross, as if cowering at its mercy, coiled a black serpent.

Down they continued, finding it hard to believe their eyes. They moved past the castle walls until the ponies came to a soft landing on the narrow cobbled street outside the castle gate. The street stretched crookedly away into the distance, with gable-topped houses and shops closely grouped together.

The guards stood aside to let the party pass beneath the portcullis, and they followed the Frenchman inside. As Dan gathered all the ponies, leading them away across the courtyard, the children found themselves flanked by knights, who proceeded to escort them through a crowd of people towards the Great Hall. *They are all dressed like characters in a history book*, thought Jo, her eye drawn towards a blacksmith who was fashioning a sword out of gleaming metal heated in the fire. Jake noticed a boy of about his own age chasing another lad, dodging amongst the crowd.

James marched, his eyes fixed on the elaborately carved door towards which they were heading. Everything seemed to be so normal, yet here he was in the middle of the night with his brother and sister, several fathoms below the sea's surface in broad daylight and surrounded by folk from a bygone age!

"Where on earth are we?" he asked the Frenchman. They were now inside the Great Hall, where shafts of light from the slender windows illuminated the tall stone columns rising up to a high arched roof. Three long tables filled the aisle, and the children found themselves seated amongst the band of knights who had accompanied them down through the sea and into this ancient castle. The gentle sound of a harp drifted soothingly around the hall.

"In the Court of Sir Tristram, Lord of Lyonesse," came the reply. Jake was about to question what he meant, but the Frenchman continued. "Once he was governor of all Cornwall and had jurisdiction over the western lands from his seat at Tintagel, before he was called here to the lost land of Lyonesse."

"Why Lyonesse?" asked Jo.

"You will have heard about the legend of Atlantis?"

"The ancient city which disappeared beneath the sea? Does it really exist?" asked James enthusiastically. "I thought it was just a myth."

"You are in the heart of Atlantis as we speak, for Atlantis is the capital of Lyonesse."

Before the Frenchman could explain any further the history of Atlantis and Lyonesse, a loud fanfare announced the entrance of Sir Tristram, causing a respectful hush to descend on the assembled throng. He was preceded by a lady whose dazzling dress shone even in the shadows of the hall. Her flowing blue robe was inlaid with a braid of sapphires, emeralds, and rubies, and her jet-black hair, which was beneath a simple white bonnet, hung down to the small of her back. Her azure eyes sparkled brightly as she surveyed the crowd and focused closely on the new arrivals. *She could almost be the queen of the mermaids*, thought Jake, whose imagination was once again getting the better of him.

"Lady Isabelle," explained the Frenchman, "Sir Tristram's cousin."

As Lady Isabelle took her seat, Sir Tristram placed himself on the throne beside her. He was a tall, striking figure with a short greying beard and broad shoulders, from which draped his regal cape of lambswool. His purple gown was fastened by a gold medallion.

The third member of the group had a simple grey skullcap on his head, yet he had an air of nobility and wisdom about him that justified his place amongst such exalted company. He had a long, pointed white beard, and his hair fell thickly onto his shoulders. The man wore a black gown decorated with strange patterns embroidered in silver braid. Closer inspection revealed these to be the signs of the zodiac. His prominent nose resembled the beak of an eagle, prompting Jake to think of him as a birdman, and his eyes seemed as dark as ebony.

"Sir Tristram." It was the Frenchman who broke the silence. "I present the three who bear the silent bell—and with it, the piece that gives it sound."

At this, Sir Tristram leaned forward and inspected the young holidaymakers, who had found themselves caught up in this unlikely plot. Each instinctively kneeled before him. "Arise, and let it be known who you are."

"My name is Jo Briscoe, and these are my brothers, James and Jake."

"Please, sir," said James, "what is so special about the bell I found in the rocks? Ever since I took it home, weird things have been happening around us, and none of us can understand why!"

"Will you explain, please, Merlin?" requested Sir Tristram, not for a moment taking his eyes off James as though studying his reaction.

"Merlin?" exclaimed all three children together.

Jake's birdman replied, "It is a long and complicated story, but let me begin by saying I am indeed Merlin, although you may find this hard to believe."

"Impossible!" blurted out James. "Can you really be named after the wizard who lived in the days of King Arthur?" The hall echoed with laughter at this question.

"Not exactly," Merlin said with a grin. "You see, I am not named after the wizard at all. I am the *same* Merlin you may have read about in stories. It was I who looked after the unknown young son of Uther Pendragon, and when the boy became Arthur, King of the Britons, it was I who remained at his side to advise him."

"Wow! Unreal!" uttered Jake. His brother and sister remained speechless. There didn't seem anything else to say.

"You asked for an explanation," said Merlin, about whose identity there was no longer any doubt. "Let me begin by warning you the world is in grave danger. It is in much greater danger than you could imagine— beyond the understanding of those who sit in government." This reference to the world above the sea came as a surprise to the children. "Your father is caught up in a political situation that is not unusual, but there are forces at work which are far more powerful than human greed and weaponry. Governments can deal in arms and diplomacy, but they cannot compete with sorcery."

The children gasped and gathered closer to one another, thinking of their father's return to London. James asked how sorcery could be involved in politics. Merlin paused to think about his response before continuing.

"A very long time ago, during the Dark Ages, the Round Table was established in the name of right, and King Arthur's knights patrolled the land to ensure that good prevailed over evil. Their influence spread far and wide, and knights from other lands travelled to Britain to take their place at the table. You have already met one such knight today."

Brothers and sister looked at one another in amazement before redirecting their gaze to Merlin.

"Stand forward, Sir Lancelot du Lac!"

"Enchanté, mes amis. À votre service." This was the Frenchman who had rescued them at the cave and who had been there to meet them at the cliff's edge before bringing them to this magical kingdom beneath the waves.

"Sir Lancelot?" echoed Jake in amazement.

"All around you are others who used to sit at the Round Table: Sir Gawain, slayer of the Green Knight. Sir Bors and Sir Percival, who shared in the sacred Quest for the Holy Grail with the noble Sir Galahad." Merlin continued to introduce several more knights and finished by summoning the harpist. "This is Sir Lamorak. Do not be fooled by the gentle sound of the harp, for he is one of the fiercest men in battle."

Sir Gawain stepped forward and bowed before kneeling in front of Jo as a token of vowing to protect her from evil. In olden times, the Knights of the Round Table had staked their reputations on service to king and country and, above all, the protection of maidens in the face of danger.

"Good knights, I would be honoured to come under your protection." Her words resulted in further bowing on the part of the men around her, and she blushed as she continued. "Firstly, how can the world's problems be solved from this secret ancient city at the bottom of the sea? Secondly, what has this bell got to do with it?"

"Where there is good, there must also be evil." This was the first time Lady Isabelle had spoken, and her soft, lilting voice was like no other they had ever heard. Each word seemed to hang in the air like wisps of pollen from a honeysuckle. "King Arthur's half-sister walks the earth at this time, and her power is great—too great for mortal man."

"Morgana Le Fay," added Sir Tristram with dread in his voice. "It was her evil cunning that destroyed the Round Table once before, and now she has returned to turn man against man in order to destroy the world as you know it."

"We do not know where she is now, but we can see her influence at work," added Lancelot. "She weaves her magic amongst the wildlife, and it must be her behind the threat that has been sent to your father's government."

"I don't suppose that she has power over magpies?" After receiving resigned nods of agreement, James went on to tell the story of his room being ransacked by the two birds which were probably seeking the bell.

"Show me the bell, James," commanded Merlin, who then held it aloft and marvelled at the wonderful craftsmanship which had created it. He motioned to Jo to hand over the piece that had been delivered to her windowsill. As he held the two shining trophies up, a gasp echoed around the Great Hall. "It will take the skills of a true craftsman to put this back in working condition. Send for Cabhan."

"This is all incredible," announced James. "If we weren't here at the bottom of the sea, it would be impossible to believe. Everyone will think we've gone mad. They'll lock us away!"

"Besides," Jake took up the argument, "if you really are who you say you are, where is King Arthur himself?"

"To begin with, you are to tell no one what you have seen here. If we allow you to return to your uncle's farm, you will act as though none of this has happened. Do I make myself clear?" There was a threat about the way Merlin spoke, leaving them in no doubt that he was serious, and the children meekly nodded.

"As for King Arthur, he and his queen are not amongst us in Lyonesse, but we believe that the magical echo of this bell is the key to help bring him back to lead us. Ah, here is Cabhan," said Merlin as the young blacksmith Jo had noticed on her way through the courtyard entered the hall and bowed before the wizard. When he had explained the task to Cabhan, Merlin continued. "To defeat the forces of evil, the Round Table has to be reformed, and this means awakening the king himself and those faithful knights who lie at rest with him. For this, we need to reclaim his sword, Excalibur, which once was forged for him and him alone."

"I'm sorry, Merlin," said Jo. "I'm afraid I still don't understand what this bell has to do with the Round Table."

"The history of King Arthur tells of two swords. It was decreed that the man who could draw the sword from a stone was the true son of Uther Pendragon and therefore the rightful king of Britain. No one had been able to do so until Arthur stepped forward, and the blade came away with ease."

"The second?"

"The second was Excalibur and was given to him by the Lady of the Lake."

"Ah, I remember now," said James. "When King Arthur was killed, one of his knights threw it back into the water, and a hand came up and grabbed it. That was the same hand—the Lady of the Lake's hand, that is—which had given it to him in the first place."

"That is correct," confirmed Merlin. "It was Sir Bedivere who eventually obeyed his king's command and returned Excalibur to the lake. He now also lies at rest in Avalon with his master and other noble men who served with him, Sir Gareth and Sir Galahad. The Lady herself, who dwells far beneath the lake's surface, will only rise from the depths in answer to the echo of this bell."

"Long have we been awaiting this discovery," added Sir Gawain.

"I know it's beautiful," said Jo, "but what makes it so special? I mean, why should the ring of a bell be the only way to summon the Lady of the Lake?"

There was a brief silence while all those at the top table glanced at one another. Presently, it was Lady Isabelle who replied in her lilting tones.

"The Lake is known as Dozmary Pool, which is said to be bottomless." She paused in order to see if the children understood what she was saying. "Its depths sink far beyond the imagination of man, for no man could imagine the enchanting world which appears beneath its granite bed. It is a timeless place, where mysteries of the universe unfold and where the arts of the deepest magic are practised. The Bell of Nimue was fashioned there long ago, before time on the surface of Earth began."

"Wow!" uttered Jake.

"So the bell has a name?" asked James. "The Bell of Nimue."

"Who or what is Nimue?" enquired Jo.

"Nimue is the high priestess of the land beneath the waters of Dozmary. She also goes by the name of the Lady of the Lake."

"Many legends have been told about the Bell of Nimue." Merlin said, taking up the story. "When the Great King was presented with Excalibur, he also received the bell so the Lady could be summoned to his aid if his life was threatened. It was stolen by Mordred at the Battle of Camlann."

"Mordred? I don't understand. Who's Mordred?" enquired Jake.

"Arthur's nephew, and the treacherous son of Morgana Le Fay," explained Sir Tristram. "Once, Mordred was himself a loyal subject and devout knight of the Round Table, but his mother persuaded him to rebel in the hope that *he* would become king in Arthur's place."

"So he was a traitor, then?" asked James.

"Yes. His mind was twisted by an evil spell," confirmed Sir Gawain. "He had performed many valiant deeds, and his bravery was beyond doubt, but he became like a fallen angel, siding with the devil himself, when the treachery of Morgana Le Fay turned him to commit high treason against his king and his country."

Merlin returned to the legend after a brief pause. "The Battle of Camlann signalled the end of the fairest age of time in this land. After Mordred stole the bell, it was no longer there when Arthur needed it most—when its ring would have brought the Lady's magic to his aid.

Instead, it was Mordred himself who delivered the mortal wound to the king."

"Mordred also died at Camlann, a place not far from here, and his body was thrown from the bridge into the River Camel," Merlin went on. "No one realised it at the time, but Nimue's Bell must have fallen into the river with him when he died."

"So it was washed down the stream into the estuary and finally out to sea," concluded James.

"Lost for over a thousand years," added Merlin, "until rumours spread amongst the sea fowl that it had been seen in shallow waters around Pentire Point."

"Morgana herself heard word of this, and she has sent her followers to find it," said Sir Gawain.

Jo shuddered as she thought of the men who had attacked them on the beach, and also of the moment Jake had run into the strangely dressed man at Trewinnick Cove. "Of course!" she exclaimed. "We've met them more than once. Jake, do you remember that weirdo you ran into? It must have been about the time James found the bell. And those birds watching us all the time!"

"Yes, and the way the terns stood guard over our things while we swam. They must have known the bell was in James's rucksack."

"They did indeed," said Sir Percival with a knowing smile. "And so did the raven that swooped down from the cliff."

"There seems to be something magical about the birds around here," said James. "You speak as if you were there," he added, looking at Sir Percival.

"Indeed he was," answered Sir Lancelot. "I said earlier that Morgana Le Fay held influence over the wildlife. Fortunately, so does Merlin, and we are able to visit the land disguised as seabirds."

"I didn't imagine it, then," James went on, "when I thought I saw a gold cross on the seagulls' breasts?"

"No, you were not imagining it, James," answered Merlin. "Knights of the Round Table can appear as gulls, and they bear the sign of the cross. There are many other seabirds, which are our allies, but they do not change into human form. The carrion, the ravens, and the magpies come under the evil spell of Morgana Le Fay."

OLRIC!

"Don't forget buzzards!" added Jake. "That red-eyed Olric has evil written all over him!"

"What happens now that we have the bell, Merlin?" asked James, changing the subject.

"It is your destiny to speak to the Lady. Once the bell has been repaired, you must take it to the lake and ring it from the shore so that its echoes will reach her ears through the watery depths."

"How do we find the lake?" asked Jo.

"You will find Dozmary Pool," replied Merlin, "on the southern heights of Bodmin Moor."

"Really? But why us?" asked James. "Surely this is a task for you and these warriors?"

"Today's problems must be solved by today's people. While we may cling to the past, the future should rest on your shoulders," said Merlin. "This is your destiny."

"You can depend on the reborn Knights of the Round Table to help you in this quest. Our spirits are rekindled, and we shall be there if you need us," added Sir Gawain.

At this, there was a rousing cheer which might have raised the roof of the great hall if it had not been held under fifty fathoms of the Atlantic, and the assembled knights launched into song.

> "'Twas the fairest age of time,
> When knights patrolled the land.
> Against all ill and evil will,
> We made our righteous stand.
>
> We rode at Arthur's side,
> Knights of true honour bound.
> We blazed the trail of the Holy Grail,
> And glory shone around.
>
> To a damsel in distress,
> Good knights we straightway came
> To rescue her from the evil cur
> And uphold her worthy name.

Now poor damsels weep;
The sun no longer shines.
Those glory days are but a haze
In a long-forgotten time.

But the day will surely dawn
King Arthur's court will see
Foes put to flight and men to right,
And a new world will be free."

While the great hall reverberated to the passionate singing, Cabhan returned to present the bell to Merlin, who inspected the craftsmanship that had gone into its repair. A respectful hush descended while he passed it carefully to Isabelle. "Now we are able to act," announced Sir Tristram. "The appointed three must return to the mainland before dawn catches them away from their beds. Instruct them well, Merlin. Tomorrow night they must go to Dozmary Pool, and then we shall make our stand against Morgana Le Fay. Good knights, we must take counsel."

These words were greeted with further cheering from the assembled company before the three guests were led back outside, where they found Dan waiting with their ponies.

"You will be taken back to the beach," said Merlin as they mounted the ponies. "Remember to mention nothing that has taken place tonight. Tomorrow at midnight, you must return to the cliff, and I shall be there to meet you with Nimue's Bell. You will take it across the moor to summon the Lady of the Lake." With that, Merlin turned on his heels and went back inside the Great Hall. The ponies trotted out of the courtyard, and moments later they were in the air, leaving the battlements far below.

Chapter 8

La Mirabelle

Dawn was beginning to break, casting a cold light on the hilltops in front of them as the ponies cantered over the calm waters towards the shore. Upon reaching the shallows, the young riders prepared to dismount and step onto dry sand, but each pony gathered speed once more, and they stayed put as the ponies made for the cliff. On the way across the uneven surface, their attention was drawn to a familiar hunched figure entering the cave where they had been attacked the previous day.

"Hey! There's Hilda! Do you think she's seen us?" asked Jo anxiously.

"I hope not," answered James, "but we'd better get back before she does. It would be good to know why she's snooping about so early, wouldn't it?"

"I bet she'd have a few questions to ask about where we've been as well," added Jake.

"All the more reason to get ourselves back to bed," said Jo.

"I don't trust that woman. Hey, do you think she might be Morgana Le Fay? She could easily be a witch, couldn't she?"

"You shouldn't jump to conclusions, Jake, but I have to agree with you. I can't stand her either!"

"That's decided, then," said Jo. "Not often we all agree, is it?"

At the end of the line of tamarisks, the ponies stopped. When the children had dismounted, Dan led them galloping away inland, leaving their riders to walk the remaining distance to the farmhouse.

After entering the kitchen, the children swiftly quietened the dogs, who greeted them enthusiastically, before they were stopped in their tracks. James swallowed hard, preparing himself for coming up with an explanation. Staring at him from a chair by the Aga was a pair of flashing angry eyes: somehow, Hilda had got back before them!

Professor Egbert Head was under pressure. He had been up working all night. He was unaccustomed to meeting deadlines, and this was a deadline he simply had to meet—under pain of death. He looked every bit the mad professor who had dedicated his entire life to research: elderly, short-sighted, and red-faced beneath thinning white hair. Although he was nearly six foot tall, he looked a lot shorter owing to a stoop acquired through many years of toiling at various laboratory desks since his days at Cambridge University. He had no family, so he was always available to anyone who needed his knowledge and his brilliance in the field of quantum physics.

His real name was Edward Headley, but he had been nicknamed Egghead in his early schooldays. This later evolved into Egbert Head, and the name had stuck ever since. Home to the professor was a modest flat in South London, but he was seldom there, owing to his talents being much in demand. Companies all over the world had hired his expertise, and he was always happy to work in return for a roof over his head and the supply of regular meals, accompanied by a nice tipple of Scotch whisky.

He had never been concerned whether his work was for honest industry or for criminal organisations. His current employer treated him as well as any other, although he knew that failure would not be acceptable and the consequences would be dire. He shuddered while thinking about his present boss, hoping he would be able to solve the problem soon. Then he could return to the relative comfort of his flat. His task was to track the path of a comet, establish control over it, and propel it towards Earth.

"Well, Professor?"

"I am experimenting with the introduction of a revised formula, through applying fx to the power of four, which ought to subject the area to a stronger gravitational pull."

"Let us hope you are correct, Professor."

"Really, Jake, you are so irresponsible," lectured Jo, entering the kitchen and discovering Hilda already there. "You'll have to explain yourself to Uncle Matty when he gets up."

"Good morning, Hilda," said James, putting on a friendly act. "You're up very early."

Hilda got to her feet, her hands on her hips, and she scowled back before replying angrily. "I wonder why the three of you are coming into the house at this time? You should never leave the house without asking me or your uncle!"

"No, but ..." started Jake.

"It was all Jake's fault, really. James came into my room and woke me up to say he'd disappeared, so we both went out and looked for him. It's a good job we found him, but he's going to be in real trouble now."

While this charade had been taking place, Jake had quickly realised his sister had managed to invent an ingenious alibi. The problem now was for him to be equally quick in thinking of a reason for his alleged behaviour. He realised everyone was looking at him and awaiting a response. "I just couldn't sleep, so I decided to go down to do some fishing off the rocks. I thought I could give Uncle a treat of some mackerel for breakfast."

"Your uncle would be furious if he knew that you had gone down to the shore on your own." Hilda paused, curling her mouth into a sneer. "And Jake, I do not see any fish, so where are these mackerel?"

"I never got to do any fishing because these two caught up with me first."

Jo could have hugged her little brother for dreaming up such a convincing story. Despite this, she did feel guilty about so many lies being told.

"And the fishing line?"

"I took it off him and left it just outside." This time the lie came from James, who had sensed Jake was floundering. Fortunately he knew the line was indeed outside the back door, because their mother had insisted it was put there rather than taking it into the house.

"I do hope it wasn't us who woke you up, Hilda," said Jo with mock concern. "It is terribly early, isn't it?"

"No, I always wake at this time. I heard nothing until I came downstairs to find you coming through the kitchen door, and I am very angry with all of you. You must go back to your rooms."

Now she's lying too, thought Jo. *She really does give me the creeps.*

What was she doing on the beach then? thought James.

How did she get back before us? wondered Jake, although he was beginning to work out a possible answer to this following her disappearance the previous evening.

"It's certainly back to bed for you, Jake," said Jo. "With a bit of luck, James will throttle you with your blinking fishing line."

"Don't give him any ideas!" protested Jake.

"Don't tempt me," added James, shepherding his younger brother out of the kitchen and up the stairs, closely followed by his sister. Once on the landing, they all paused for a brief whispered conversation, their hearts beating furiously. They agreed to not discuss the events of the night, in particular the last few minutes, until later in the morning, when they could be sure they wouldn't be overheard.

Hilda stood looking out of the window, her face expressionless. She did not believe Jake had been out fishing, but she could not imagine any other reason why the children had been outside at such an hour. The time on the kitchen clock was ten past six.

"I'd given you up," said Matty as his three bleary-eyed young lodgers entered the kitchen. "A couple of days' sea air, and you can't get out of bed!"

So Uncle Matty didn't know about their earlier meeting with Hilda. Either he had not seen her, or she had chosen to not tell him about their meeting in the early hours.

"Oh, Uncle, we had no idea it was so late. Look, boys, it's nearly half past ten!" said Jo.

"Better grab a quick bowl of cereal," said Matty. "I've arranged a treat for this morning." He paused for a reaction. "You'll never guess what." The 3Js looked at one another but said nothing before looking back at their uncle. "Madame Lafayette is going to take us out on her yacht." This news was greeted with squeals of delight. "You must get a move on, or we shall miss the tide."

When the dinghy pulled up alongside *La Mirabelle* off Daymer Bay, the yacht was a lot bigger than she had looked from the shore. In all, she measured ninety feet from bow to stern, with a beam of twenty-two feet. A line of portholes in the hull showed there were lots of cabins, and two upper decks provided plenty of space above, the bridge giving a commanding view to all sides through tinted reinforced glass. It was a luxury vessel that was clearly seaworthy in the face of all weathers.

Today, the weather was perfect for cruising. There was very little wind, and the sea was a shimmering calm, its deep blue reflecting the clear sky above. Now approaching midday, the sun was burning down, and there was a light breeze as the yacht began to motor out to sea, her bow cutting through the water and the engine throbbing quietly below decks.

Madame Lafayette, now dressed more suitably for sailing, had introduced her crew in a manner associated with royalty, and Jo had felt like a princess as each crewman bowed before her. Matty was struck by the small number of crew needed to sail such a large vessel; in all, there were six. The captain's name was Anders, and the other men were Jose, Fernando, Karl, and Mikael. The solitary woman was Bergita, an efficient-looking Italian who prepared meals in the galley.

The yacht increased her speed while the guests were given a conducted tour of the upper decks, the galley, and the luxurious salon, as Madame Lafayette called it, which was her base for resting and entertaining. The crew evidently had a lot of space for their own relaxation. Not even the owner would expect to enter this area without an invitation, so it came as no surprise that her guests were not invited in there either.

"First, we shall go out to sea to show you how fast we can go. Then we shall come back and idle along the coastline, so you can see what it looks like from the water," announced Madame Lafayette.

"Sounds a cracking idea to me," said Matty enthusiastically.

The sun was shining brightly, and back on the shore, holidaymakers would be seeking shade to keep out of its glare. The movement of the yacht provided a refreshing breeze for her passengers. While gazing back at the rapidly shrinking cliffs, James's mind flickered between this magnificent modern yacht and the ancient world of Lyonesse somewhere in the depths below. Meanwhile, Jo's mind was back on her pony galloping over the waves towards them. Of the three, only Jake was living for this moment of

La Mirabelle

luxury, enjoying the smooth pace of *La Mirabelle* as she sliced her course out to sea. Even he was reminded of his recent experience when he caught sight of a flock of seabirds a stone's throw off the port bow, while another flock flew behind the stern, crying noisily in search of food. *I wonder …* he thought.

Professor Egbert Head had taken a long time to drift off to sleep. He had found the night's work difficult and unrewarding, especially because his employer had been so impatient and unappreciative of his recent efforts.

At midday, he should have been in his deepest slumbers, but even his sleep was disturbed by visions of extraterrestrial combat, asteroids and meteorites colliding with cataclysmic force under the direction of complex mathematical formulae. He dreamed about a comet disappearing from the universe under an inexplicable antigravitational pull while a colossal tidal wave was on the verge of devouring him. When he woke up, his forehead was drenched in sweat.

It was late afternoon when *La Mirabelle* cruised round Pentire Point, past Polzeath and on to Daymer Bay, where it dropped anchor. It had been a great day out on the luxury yacht, which had taken them out to sea and returned close to the coast past Boscastle, Tintagel, and Port Isaac. They had seen dolphins, seals, and all kinds of seabirds. They had been made wonderfully welcome by all the crew, who had gone out of their way to involve them in all their routine tasks.

Madame Lafayette herself had been such a joy that her guests found it difficult to say goodbye as they parted with many a *merci beaucoup, au revoir,* and *à bientôt* on the quayside. She had spent time with each of the children, hearing about their likes and dislikes, their escapades at school, and what they liked to do when they stayed with their uncle at his farm. So enchanting was her company that the 3Js resolved to devote more of their energy to studying French when they returned to school the following month.

OLRIC!

Back at the farm, they gathered in the barn to discuss the previous night. All their minds had been fully distracted by their day on *La Mirabelle*, but now they each wanted to air their thoughts, especially about their brush with Hilda in the early hours.

"You were brilliant with that story of me sneaking out, Jo."

"It was the way you carried it on, though. Even I started to believe you'd gone fishing. And then the way James managed to round it off! Yes, it was a brilliant team effort."

"Absolutely!" agreed James. "I'd like to know what Hilda was up to, and she never even told Uncle Matty about us. It's as if she didn't want him to know how early she got up."

"And how did she get back before us? That's what I'd like to know."

"Jo, I think I may know the answer to that," said Jake. Two pairs of ears listened agog as he went on to tell them about the previous evening when Hilda had seemed to vanish while his back had been turned.

"So you think there may be a secret passage from the dining room?"

"It's not by any means out of the question," said James. "We know smugglers used to bring goods into houses using such tunnels to avoid being seen by the coastguard."

"But it's so far!"

"Think about it, Jo. The path takes you along the side of a field and round the headland before you get to the beach isn't nearly so far as the crow flies."

"Or the mole burrows," added Jake, earning a raised eyebrow from his brother.

"Okay," admitted Jo, "but there's obviously something very suspicious about Hilda. She must be Morgana Le Fay, mustn't she?"

"Certainly looks like a witch."

"Spot on, Jake!" said James. "Besides, if she *is* a witch, she can probably appear and disappear where she likes."

"Which means …" started Jake.

"She could be here right now, listening to our conversation." They all looked around anxiously.

"No, she isn't. She's just come out of the house," said James. "There she is. Someone ought to follow her." He looked at Jake.

"I reckon we all follow her. Well, not exactly follow," cut in Jo. "If we split up and go to various vantage points, she'll be in someone's view all the time, but it won't look as though she's being followed."

"Good idea, Jo. You stay here up on the hay bales. Jake, you go up the hill towards the headland, and I'll keep an eye on the lane and the fields down to the village."

Before she could reply, both boys had abandoned her and gone to their lookout posts. *Why do they take all the exciting jobs? It was my idea, after all.*

She didn't sulk for long, however, as the chance to settle back and stretch out in the fresh, sweet-smelling hay was an attractive one after the rigours of the last few days. She might have dozed off, but her mind was buzzing with questions about knights and witches, underwater cities, luxury yachts, and ponies. Above all the other excitements of the holiday so far, nothing could surpass the exhilaration she had felt riding bareback over the waves. She could see herself entering the ring at the East Sussex Show, then flying gracefully over the jumps before collecting her winner's rosette in front of her beaming parents in the grandstand.

Parents! Jo felt guilty that she had not spared them so much as a fleeting thought, and she wondered whether her mother had got home safely and whether her father was managing to cope with his complicated job in parliament. Being in government seemed boring to her, and she hoped he would be able to sort out whatever silly problem it was. Then they would both be able to come back to join them on holiday.

Her mind was distracted by the sight of a large bird of prey swooping overhead and then hovering motionless over the field which rose beyond the house and towards the cliffs. The memory of Olric's attack might have filled her with fear, but at least she could admire this bird from a safe distance. She marvelled at its ability to remain so still for such a long time whilst watching some unsuspecting rodent going about its business in the grass below.

Jake was lying out of sight in the golden corn, which was soon to be harvested. He had made his way stealthily uphill through the field, and he was now able to take in the view across the valley, past the farm buildings, and down the lane towards New Polzeath. He looked out into the Atlantic, framed between Stepper and Pentire Points and the rocky, uninhabited islands of Gulland and Newland. James would be down there somewhere, and he wished they had mobiles so they could keep in touch. It would be a waste of his time if his brother had already tracked Hilda down in the village.

A sudden blow to his head caused Jake to squeal, and he turned to find himself staring into the eyes of a buzzard, whose talons stretched menacingly towards his face. To his great alarm, he recognised the red eyes and plumage round its neck. He instinctively lashed out, but his flailing arms didn't make any contact with the bird, which continued to hover above him. Jake leapt to his feet and ran back downhill through the corn.

He didn't know whether he was being followed, but he dared not look round for fear of those red eyes pursuing him with merciless intent. Only fifty metres now lay between him and the barn, and he could see Jo watching him with horror across her face.

He was aware of the fluttering wings overtaking him. He looked up to see the bird swooping overhead and rising upwards to leave him approaching the safety of the barn. He did not stop running until he had climbed high up in the hay bales, where he lay panting for breath.

"Olric?" he asked as he was joined by his sister, and she nodded in agreement. There could be no mistaking that collar of red feathers. They had no further chance to discuss Jake's adventure because they were joined by a breathless James making his way up the bales.

"I saw her," he said. "I went into the beach shop and was just coming out when Hilda went past me. She was talking to Leatherjacketman, and it seemed they knew each other quite well."

"What was she talking about?"

"Did they see you?"

"No, I don't think so, and I don't know what was said. I was too far away. They were walking up the road towards Rock, and I followed as far as the Oystercatcher. Then I came back here as quickly as I could. How about you two?"

Chapter 9

Dozmary Pool

It was half past eleven when James, Jo, and Jake stole away from the house, past the row of tamarisks, and towards the cliffs. They waited, listening to the sound of the roaring surf. They looked out over the waves for any sign of knights or even seagulls who might have announced the approach of Merlin or Sir Lancelot. All they could see, however, were the twinkling lights of distant shipping and the undulating foam, a moving mass of grey in the darkness.

The moonlight shone onto the dark swell of the sea.

Someone was approaching! Jo felt her heart beating quickly, and she gasped. She was on the point of stepping out to meet him when James pulled her firmly back. At first annoyed, she realised as the man drew near that this was not the person they had expected to meet. Jo heaved a quiet sigh of relief and quietly thanked her brother for rescuing her. She shivered. She was frightened, but she was also aware of how cold it had suddenly become. Unconsciously, all three children drew their light summer fleeces around them.

They watched carefully as the man walked purposefully past them. *Leatherjacketman!* Their eyes continued to follow the familiar figure as he made his way down to the shore. Two more men emerged silently from the rocks to meet him before they all disappeared into the cave.

"What are they doing?"

"I don't know, Jo," replied James. "But they must be the enemy. Look—they're carrying something out of the cave." Sure enough, two of the men were heaving a large bundle across the sand towards the water.

OLRIC!

"What can it be?" whispered Jo. "What on earth are they carrying?"

"Treasure! Must be!" whispered Jake. "Look over there. Isn't that a boat coming in?" True enough, an inflatable with one man aboard was coming in with the surf and, as soon as it beached, the bundle was swiftly put aboard. The three men turned the dinghy round before jumping in. The inflatable bounced through the waves and powered round the point and out of sight.

"There's something very odd going on round here, and Hilda's got something to with it," said James.

"Morgana Le Fay, you mean," corrected Jo. "I bet those were the same men you saw her talking to in the village."

"Definitely. Leatherjacketman was one of them. And don't forget he was also one of those horrible men in the cave. It's hard to tell about the other two in this light, but I'll bet you anything it's the same gang."

Just then came the gentle sound of muffled hoof beats, and they were joined by three familiar ponies, which trotted up behind them. Each one nuzzled their riders of the night before, and James was surprised how confident he felt as he hugged his pony.

"Hey, look," said Jake.

"Where? I can't see anything," answered his brother.

"There. Those seagulls. They're making for us." True enough, a flock of gulls had been flying low over the water and was rising towards the clifftop. The birds circled the children and came down to land in the shadows behind a thicket of gorse. Even in the half-light, they could make out a red cross blazed on their breasts. A thin mist swirled around the birds for a moment, and in their place appeared Sir Lancelot and several other knights. None of them said a word, but behind them appeared a tall man in a black gown with patterns of glinting silver. Merlin. In his hand he held Nimue's Bell, which had a golden cord looped through the handle. There was a magical glow about it as it gleamed in the half-light of the moon.

"James, hang this bell round your neck. It will not make a sound until you hold it up and ring it over the waters of Dozmary Pool. Time is short," he said urgently. "You must hasten across the moor. These ponies know where to go, and they will take you there as swiftly as they can."

"Aren't you coming with us?" asked Jo.

James added, "And the knights? Surely Sir Lancelot …"

James's question was cut short by Merlin's reply. "No. You have to see Nimue by yourselves. When you are near the lake, the ponies will stop at the beginning of a path through the gorse. There, you must dismount and make your way along the path until you reach a flat granite rock that can only be seen from the water. If you ring the bell there, the Lady herself should appear."

"What do we say to her?" asked James. "I mean, she may not trust us."

"Explain to her that you have come on the quest to awaken the Great King and that you need his sword. Tell her it is I, Merlin, who has sent you."

"What if she doesn't believe us?" questioned Jo.

Merlin drew himself up to his full height, towering over her and fixing her with a cold stare. "She will believe you." His words were decisive.

"Right, so she gives us the sword. What do we do then?" asked Jake.

"The ponies will be waiting, and you are to return here. On no account must you stop. There are many dangers out there, and you do not know who you can trust. Speak to no one until you are back in the company of the Round Table."

With these words of warning, Merlin withdrew into the darkness with the knights, and they were alone once more. The 3Js mounted the ponies and felt themselves being carried inland, through their uncle's fields. Each hedgerow was cleared as if jumped by a steeplechaser at Cheltenham. Soon they found themselves travelling at high speed, almost flying over the Cornish countryside. From time to time, a cloud covered the moon, yet still they galloped on through the darkness, the ponies avoiding all hazards and pitfalls on the bumpy ground beneath them.

Within a few minutes, they had moved far inland, and now they were climbing. They were on the sparsely populated wilderness of Bodmin Moor, with the well-known landmarks of Rough Tor and Brown Willy, silhouetted against the stars to the east. Thickets of gorse looked dark and eerie, moving like ghostly ghouls in the swirling mist, while the occasional rock shone dimly in the half light. All of a sudden, as the children soared over a stone wall, Jake's mount lost its footing, and he was thrown onto the ground.

He was getting painfully to his feet when he realised he was staring at an enormous woolly brown face with long, pointed horns sticking out from the sides of its head. Steam seemed to be coming out of its nostrils, and it made an ominous snuffling noise as it moved towards him. Shutting his eyes in terror, Jake tried to roll away to safety, but he only succeeded in pricking himself on the gorse before he saw the beast retreating harmlessly away.

"Are you all right, Jake?" It was Jo's voice, coming from above him as she sat looking down from her pony.

"Yes, thanks," he replied, feeling a little embarrassed. "But did you see that beast? I thought it was going to eat me!"

"Obviously didn't fancy you, Jake!" laughed James. "Anyway, cattle are herbivores!"

"Didn't seem much like cattle to me! That was never a cow. Are you sure it wasn't a dragon?"

A little while later, the ponies paused for a moment behind the rocky outcrop on Garrow Hill and froze in their tracks. Their riders sensed them shivering with fear and looked out ahead of them. They could see why the ponies were scared, because they were not alone on the moor that night: about twenty figures were moving across the moor ahead of them, and there was something about their appearance that looked unfriendly. They were human in outline, yet their arms and legs seemed unusually long, and their heads looked large in relation to their torsos. Each of them carried what looked like an axe, and as they wound their way out of sight round the hill, the 3Js remained in the shelter of the rocks, their hearts beating furiously.

"Who do you think they are?" asked Jo nervously.

"I don't know," whispered James. "Whoever or whatever they are, I don't like the look of them one bit."

"They could be goblins," whispered Jake, trembling all over. "Did you see the axes they were carrying?"

"Do you think it's safe to move yet?" asked Jo even more nervously than before.

James cautiously moved forward to look round the rocks to see if the coast was clear. "Come on," he said. "They seem to have gone." The ponies began to move and gathered speed once more, galloping downhill past gorse thickets and great boulders—all of which might have provided hiding places for nasty creatures of the dark. But they continued to travel safely across the lonely, rugged wastes of the moor. Jo was in the lead, enjoying the excitement of the ride, until she pulled up sharply, causing her brothers to do the same.

"What is it, Jo?" asked James.

"I don't know. It looks like a line of trees ahead of us, but I think I saw something moving."

"Shh. Listen!" said Jake in a low voice. "Do you hear that?"

"Sounds like running water," said James. "And you're right about the trees. This must be the Delank River, which flows down the moor to join the River Camel. I don't think there's anything moving apart from the branches. It's quite windy up here. Let's go on."

"I hope you're right," said Jo as she followed her brother down towards the trees. James had been right about the Delank, and a little farther downstream was Delphy Bridge, which had been built in Saxon times out of huge granite boulders. The ponies paused to drink from the stream while James kept a careful watch for anything that might be lurking ahead. The stream bubbled its way noisily under the bridge, its water black as the darkest night, contrasting with its foaming creamy froth around the stones.

When the ponies had drunk enough, the party crossed the bridge and made its way rapidly across open moorland. From the top of the next hill, they could see the distant lights of cars moving in opposite directions along a main road ahead. This was the A30. The children had spent so much time in fantasy that they had forgotten the reality of normal life, and although it was well past midnight, there was a lot of traffic moving across the major highway in and out of North Cornwall. Jamaica Inn was lit up to their left as the ponies bore them down the slope in the direction of Dozmary Pool.

The folk of Lyonesse had not witnessed such activity for many a year. Armour was being polished and weapons sharpened. Everywhere there were people at work checking buckles and making sure the army was fit to do battle against the enemy. The sounds of metal hammering against metal and the excited chattering of men and women filled the air.

Lady Isabelle oversaw preparation of the banners and flags that would accompany the army. Sir Tristram himself supervised the knights as they practised their swordsmanship. Sir Lancelot gathered a special force with an urgent errand in the coming hours, and along with Merlin, they would be travelling to the mainland.

The water rippled a ghostly white reflection of the half moonlight when the riders paused for a moment to gaze over the lake. A quarter of a mile still lay ahead of them, and they cautiously peered around them to see that they were not being followed. An owl hooted in the distance, and they were startled by a sudden movement to their right when a fox broke from its cover and stole away into the night.

"That gave me quite a fright!" admitted Jo, sweeping her hair back with her left hand.

"Come on, then," said James. "The coast seems to be clear." The ponies quietly trotted along the path while their riders continued to look warily around them.

"Look over there," said Jake suddenly.

"Where?" enquired his brother and sister together.

"There, up on that rock ahead, about twenty metres away." It was clearly visible now: standing out against the dark sky was the even darker shape of a bird, which appeared to be watching them. Jo shuddered, thinking back to the recent attacks from Olric, but at least this was not a buzzard.

"It's a raven," declared James. Although he sounded his usual knowledgeable self, he was a little unnerved. "I don't like it. They say a raven is a sign of bad luck."

"Oh," replied Jake as the bird flapped its wings and flew off in the direction of the lake. The wind had dropped, and all they could hear was the gentle thud of the ponies' hooves carrying them closer to the lake. They veered off the track onto a narrow path leading through a thick forest of prickly gorse. The gorse was high enough to hide the lake, which was only a stone's throw away on the left. They entered a clearing, and the ponies stopped.

"This must be where we get off," said James, looking around him. "Merlin told us the ponies would lead us to a path."

"There it is!" Jake pointed to a narrow space between two prickly gorse bushes. If it was a path, it was seldom trodden, but it might have occasionally been used by fishermen making their way to the shore. On dismounting, the children made their way gingerly through the gorse, and their trusted ponies grazed patiently behind them. The full expanse of Dozmary Pool opened up before them, and as they emerged from the undergrowth, they realised they were standing on the flat granite rock of which Merlin had spoken.

They looked at one another in silence and then back at the water, which lapped softly against the reeds surrounding the lake. So much had happened since they had arrived at Polzeath, yet here they were on the threshold of reawakening the legend of a mythical lady who had not appeared to man for over a thousand years. They were all alone beside the peaceful water, except for the forbidding presence of the raven, which was now perched on a rock at the water's edge about thirty metres away on their left. Jake was about to speak when the stillness was broken by a flurry of activity. A flock of geese took off noisily and flew past, low over the water, their wings beating and their throats honking. The raven remained motionless, and if the children had been closer, they might have noticed that its eyes were fixed on them.

While the surface settled back to flat calm, James slipped the silver cord over his head, and the three of them looked at the glinting bell in awe and anticipation. The excitement at the prospect of seeing the Lady of the Lake was suddenly overwhelming.

"Go on, James. Ring it!" urged Jo.

He felt a little bashful as he raised the bell, held it over the water, and shook it in front of him. It rang, but it was not what they had expected. The sound was much deeper than any of them had imagined. It sounded more like Big Ben than a little hand bell, and its peal echoed around the hills. Even more astonishing was what they saw. Thin shafts of light shot down like lasers from the stars, and the surface of the water became a kaleidoscope of ever-changing colours. The echoes evolved into a new sound quite unlike anything they had heard before, a sighing melody of harmonious voices hanging in the gentle breeze like soft strands of candy floss as a light mist descended over the lake.

As they attempted to take in the scene, they saw the source of this angelic sound emerging from the misty centre of the lake, where figures were drifting effortlessly across the surface towards the shore. At first it appeared to be another flock of geese, but after advancing closer, the figures moved like a troupe of elegant ballerinas guarding their queen in their midst.

The Lady of the Lake had answered the call of the magic bell.

They stood wide-eyed in dumbfounded amazement as she glided in white robes amongst her emerald green escort towards the granite rock. She stopped and stood on the water, her robes and satin shoes remaining completely dry in spite of their touching the surface. When she spoke, her words were uttered in a deep slow drawl, holding her audience bewitched. "Who calls me from the deep caverns that lie beneath the waters?"

For a moment they were too tongue-tied to speak at all, but then James managed to splutter a response. "James. This is my sister, Jo, and my brother, Jake."

For a long moment, time stood still as she surveyed the three children standing before her. Each of them averted their gaze because they did not have the courage to look into her deep blue eyes, which seemed capable of turning them to stone. Meanwhile, her escort silently surrounded the rock on which they stood.

"How came you by the bell that was fashioned beyond the powers of mortal man?" There was a pause as she looked at each face in turn.

James was hesitant as he uttered a nervous reply. "I found it amongst the rocks at Trewinnick Cove."

Jo said, "And a bird brought the missing part to my windowsill."

"So the magic still lives among the wildfowl ..... but that does not explain why you have come to summon me here at Dozmary."

"We have been sent by Merlin," said Jo.

"Ah, Merlin. So the wizard still weaves his magic above the ground?"

"Yes," said Jake. This was the first time that he'd spoken in the presence of the Lady. "And Sir Tristram of Lyonesse, and Sir Lancelot, and ..."

"Hush, my child. Do not speak too much. So Merlin has sent you. For what purpose?" The abrupt manner in which this question was put surprised the children, who recoiled in awe.

Despite the power of the Lady's glare, James summoned the courage to step forward, and now he looked her in the eye. "We've been sent to ask for the sword that once belonged to King Arthur."

"Excalibur," piped Jake, who for the second time might have wished he'd remained quiet, because the rock shook and the laser beams flashed like lightning.

"Never use that name lightly!"

"Sorry," muttered Jake, rather wishing he was swallowed up by the granite.

"So what causes Merlin to ask for the great sword? Such requests are not made unless there is need."

Jake remained quiet while his brother and sister told the story of the past few days. They spoke in detail about the mysterious disappearance of Lola Mendes, the attack by the men outside the cave, and the buzzard Olric. They described their rescue and the ride to Lyonesse, where they had been told about Morgana Le Fay. This led to the sinister actions of Hilda and her involvement with the villains in the village, the same men they had watched that night setting out to sea with the strange cargo from the cave.

They spoke too of their parents and Uncle Matty, which led them to describe their happy meeting with Madame Lafayette and the trip on *La Mirabelle*. Finally, they explained about their father being a minister in government and his recall to London owing to the political crisis, which even James did not fully understand.

All the while, the Lady and her bodyguard of damsels—this was how she referred to her escort—listened closely. It was only when the children had finished that she made any response.

"Your world is indeed in peril," she said, "and it is ill news that Morgana has returned. She has great power and has always been eager to use it to evil purpose. Much responsibility is resting on your shoulders. As Merlin told you himself when he sent you to me, some demands are beyond even his power.

"The king sleeps in Avalon's vale, and he will only be woken if his sword is taken to him. The sword that was forged in the lands beneath this lake has been cared for here since he was defeated by the treachery of his half-sister and her son, Mordred. Now he will have the chance to reap his revenge."

Without another word, she turned and glided back to the centre of the lake where, surrounded by her damsels. She vanished, sinking slowly beneath the surface. The laser beams disappeared, clouds covered the moon and stars, and darkness returned to Dozmary. There was silence, apart from the rustle of the reeds. The raven still watched them from its rocky perch.

"What do we do now?" asked Jake, speaking for the first time in ages.

"We wait," replied James.

"She hasn't said goodbye," mused Jo.

They waited, staring out across the water until they began to wonder whether they should return empty-handed or ring the bell once more. After all that had happened since their arrival at Penmarrett, they could not go back across the moor without the one thing they had come to collect. They didn't want to give up on their errand now. But if they rang the bell, the Lady might be annoyed by their impatience. Jake in particular had no wish to anger her any more.

Then the scene changed. Beams of light returned from the stars above, and all shone down at a precise spot in the centre of the lake. Lightning danced behind the hilltops, and a clap of thunder resounded like a whiplash as the surface of the water was broken into a golden ripple. A silver blade rose twinkling into the light, and then the Lady's hand appeared, gripping its hilt. Soon she had risen totally above the water and drifted towards them once more, holding the magnificent sword, Excalibur, above her.

The blade seemed to reflect all the colours that decorated the water, which gradually became crimson, making Excalibur look as though it was stained in the blood of battle. The damsels followed their lady, and when she stopped before the awestruck children, they spread out in a crescent behind her.

The Lady of the Lake held Excalibur in front of her with her left hand supporting the blade and her right hand open, showing the hilt, which was inlaid with jewels. Nothing was said as one of her damsels stepped forward to take the sword and place it in its magnificent leather scabbard, which was decorated with gold strands and studded with sapphires. Two other damsels wrapped the scabbard in a cream silk shroud woven with goose down before returning it to the outstretched hands of their mistress.

"James, Jo, and Jake, to you I entrust Excalibur, which must be taken to awaken the Great King from sleep in Avalon. It is made for him and him alone. Let this be a warning that if anyone other than King Arthur himself wields this sword in battle, he or she will die. You will face many dangers as you return across the moor. This sword is heavy, but I shall put a spell over it so that you will not feel its weight as long as you keep it wrapped in its hallowed shroud. When you return, you must go straight to Merlin, entrust it to his care, and recite to him these words:

> Seek the eagle as before
> When moonlight sweeps across the Tor.
> There will be pointed,
> As Joseph anointed,
> The Chalice as told in folklore."

Her words seemed to hang in the air like threads of gossamer before she continued. "Now, you must go. The bell is to be returned to the lake so it may be kept safely away from evil hands."

After presenting the bell to the leading damsel, James took the sword in his outstretched hands, and indeed he could hardly feel its weight. He looked up to speak but saw that the Lady of the Lake had already turned her back and was floating away in the company of her damsels. The water was now of the deepest blue, and the laser beams had gone. Upon reaching the middle of the lake, the Lady sank gracefully below the surface, and the last that was seen of her was the faintest wave of her hand. The deepest blue turned to grey.

The sword-bearers remained standing enthralled, their eyes fixed on the ripples where the Lady had disappeared. Many strange things had happened over the past few days, yet this mystical experience had been even more enchanting than their ride to Lyonesse. There had been something supernatural about the Lady of the Lake, something about her that transcended the passing of time, as if her attention to life on the surface of Earth was only a small part of a vast tapestry of interests across the universe.

"Cool or what?" said Jake eventually.

"Well, guys, I guess it's time to go," announced James, turning his back on the lake. Jo remained to have a final glance over the water before she followed her brothers through the reeds. Nobody noticed the raven had flown away. As they emerged from the gorse, they found their three ponies where they had left them, and soon they were galloping back towards the coast.

Chapter 10

Morgana Le Fay

A light mist descended onto the moor, which made the return journey all the more difficult to see where they were going. Yet the ponies had no difficulty in steering a constant path towards the north-west. As they approached Delphy Bridge, the eerie silence was broken by a blood-curdling screech, which stopped them in their tracks. The ponies became unsettled and restless, shivering beneath their frightened riders

"What was that?" asked Jake nervously. There was no time for a reply before their way was blocked by about twenty of the figures they had seen from Garrow Hill. Close up, they were a menacing sight. They were tall and gangly, and their faces were obscured in black hoods, from which red eyes peered out at their prey. They snorted as they advanced, and a horrible smell floated from their grotesque bodies. In their long, sinewy arms, they wielded lethal axes.

James's hands closed around the hilt of Excalibur, still concealed in its carefully wrapped shroud. *If anyone other than King Arthur himself wields this sword in battle, he will die.* He reluctantly released his grip, but death appeared to be the most likely outcome in any case as the hideous troop advanced towards them, waving their axes in well-rehearsed ritual. They gradually moved forward in a crescent, chanting their grotesque battle cry, "engulzaya motakaya, birmintauza!"

Hopelessly outnumbered and defenceless, the children were petrified and remained in a frozen stupor on the backs of the ponies. The first axe swung only a few feet in front of James's pony, which reared up in the face of its attacker. James clung onto his pony, and it took all his strength to remain on board. Jake was dragged down to the ground by a hairy, outstretched arm, and he was aware in his terror of the burning red eyes and the foul stench of the creature's breath as it pinned him down.

While his pony fled in panic, Jake screamed and punched wildly, trying to break loose, but the hold was too strong, and his energy ebbed away. Even if he had been able to free himself, two more monsters towered over him, and all he could do was wait for the inevitable end.

James was surrounded by the creatures, and they closed in, axes raised above their loathsome heads. He screamed at them, meaningless words in the face of such inhuman monsters. Even so, it gave him some courage to think he might scare them away. In fact, he'd never felt so scared in his life.

Jo had managed to urge her mount to charge forward, surprising her enemies, but now they had rallied. As she lashed out with her left hand, she was gripped by the hair, and she screamed more in fright than in pain. She was pulled from the pony, landed heavily on the ground, and was almost asphyxiated by the reeking smell as her assailant breathed over her. She was then astonished to see it turn away and flee back towards the bridge. Surprise turned to amazed relief when she saw all the other figures retreating in chaos, leaving Jake able to regather his strength. James, still on his pony, held the priceless enshrouded sword.

After clambering to his feet, Jake looked back to see the cause of their release: a flock of beautiful white swans flying down the hill behind them, the tips of their wings almost touching the ground. On their backs, the swords of warriors flashed in the moonlight as the graceful birds whistled past in pursuit of the axe-wielding ghouls. The riders hunted each of them down, hacking them ruthlessly to death, bodies evaporating into a smoking pile of groaning, decaying flesh.

After the task was completed, the posse dismounted and walked back to the children, who had watched the spectacle in a blend of shock, fear, and relief. The Briscoes were surprised to see that their rescuers were a lot smaller than the defeated enemy. They recognised the leader as one of the damsels in the Lady of the Lake's escort, and all her company were dressed in the green robes of Dozmary Pool.

The 3Js stepped forward and began to blurt out their thanks, but the leading damsel replied by holding her arm up as a signal for silence. "You must hasten on your way, for there are many perils on the moor tonight.

OLRIC!

We shall accompany you up to the Garrow, whence you shall make your own way to the coast." She murmured something in a strange, lilting language, and they were astonished to see three swans emerging to stand beside them while the ponies were led away. Some damsels gently placed the children on the swans' backs, and they sank exhausted into the soft feathers.

A moment later, the great wings came to life, and they took off, flying effortlessly past the smouldering remains of their would-be slayers. Jo looked down, recalling the hideous face and the stench that came from it when she had lain at its mercy only moments before.

The rhythmic sound of the wings beating through the night air was both beautiful and exhilarating as they rose higher into the dark sky. While passing over the wooded glade that concealed the Delank, they talked with the leading damsel, whose name was Aerhwana. Like The Lady herself, her voice had a lilting tone that floated magically over the moor. She explained she had been sent with her guards when the Lady had received word of their impending plight from a skein of geese which had seen the attack developing from their lofty position in the sky.

At the top of Garrow Hill, they paused and sat on the rocks to survey the mist-covered moorland over which the swans had flown, and it was a relief to see no sign of pursuit, apart from the ponies being ridden up from the valley by three damsels, their green robes billowing behind.

"What were those creatures?" Jo asked Aerhwana as they stood gazing into the mist. "They would have killed us, wouldn't they?"

"That I do not know. I think they would more likely have taken you prisoner and led you to their leader, Morgana Le Fay, to face questions about your part in this quest. It is the sword she craves, but you might have other answers that would be of interest to her. The creatures are moorogwyths, to give them their full title, but it's simpler to know them as moorogs. They are servants of darkness who delight in destruction."

"Horrible things," said Jo, shivering. "Thanks to you, we have nothing to fear from them now."

"Alas, you cannot count on that. There are many more moorogs ready to answer the summons of evil, and there are worse perils—more ruthless servants of darkness—that roam the land."

The children groaned, and it was Jake who put their thoughts into words. "Oh, no! There can't be *anything* worse than that, can there?"

"Can't you come with us, Aerhwana, at least as far as the coast?" implored James.

Aerhwana replied, "This is a mission that can only be undertaken by yourselves." Merlin had said something similar earlier that night. "Besides, dawn is soon breaking over the moor, and we must return to the lake before sunrise."

While she spoke, there was a familiar, comforting snort as their three trusted ponies were led to the top of the hill. They seemed none the worse for their meeting with the moorogs, and they happily nuzzled their riders

"Farewell, brave children," continued Aerhwana. "I hope we shall meet again in happier times when your quest is fulfilled."

Without another word, she turned and, followed by her escort, flew across the valley on their swans in arrow formation and out of sight. The children watched them fade into the eerie half-light before looking at one another, resigned to the knowledge that they were now alone. They turned to face the west.

"Come on," said James. "We don't want Uncle Matty to find we're not there for breakfast." Breakfast seemed a remote possibility, yet they remounted the ponies, who seemed to be much calmer after the victory over the moorogs, and swiftly rode back across the moor. All the time, they were alert to any sound or movement that might spell danger, but their return was remarkably uneventful, and their spirits rose when they reached the edge of the moor and could see the grey sea in the distance.

Gradually, as they drew closer, they could see the line of a hedge in front of them, and the ponies slowed to trot calmly towards it. On the other side, they would find the cliff and the welcoming figure of Merlin, his arms outstretched to receive Excalibur. Their spirits rose in anticipation of being greeted as heroes, like knights of bygone days returning in triumph from battle.

Their high spirits, however, were short-lived.

Upon approaching the hedge, they found it was not a hedge after all but hundreds of moorogs in a line rising as one, their axes held aloft in mocking salute. They were shouting a hideous, cackling challenge in some vile inhuman tongue. The noise was deafening, and the whole cliff shook

OLRIC!

in the din. Behind them, the sky had turned black. A dense cloud of crows came sweeping up like a vast squadron. They offered aerial support for the fiendish infantry advancing cruelly towards the three mounted children. There was no way forward.

"Oh, no! What now? We've got to get out of here," cried Jake.

"There's no way forward," shouted Jo above the noise.

"We'll have to go back. That's all we can do," said James.

"But look behind," said Jo. "They're everywhere."

"And don't they half stink," added Jake. "Look out! We're being attacked from the air as well."

Three hawks swooped low towards them, causing the ponies to rear up and flee, throwing their riders off and leaving them scrambling painfully on the ground while the encircling horde of moorogs began to close in.

"Are you two all right?" asked Jake, who had struggled to his feet.

"Come on!" yelled James. "We've got to get out of here. Let's go!"

They had no time to dwell on the bruises because escape was uppermost in their minds. Their enemies drew closer, and the children could make out the horrifying figures of the men who had attacked them at the cave. There was also a woman dressed in black, her face obscured by a veil.

"Hilda!" gasped Jo.

The crows above were now circling like a whirlwind in the darkening sky, and in its midst hovered a ferocious-looking buzzard with red eyes. Olric was poised to dive on the helpless trio.

Only twenty metres remained between the children and their enemies, who stood still. An eerie silence descended on the cliffs. The woman stepped forward and slowly removed her veil. To their horrified astonishment, it was not the face of Hilda that was exposed, and their jaws fell open in recognition of the face behind the veil. There was no mistaking the flame-red hair, even in the darkness.

There was a glow about this figure which shone as if in full light of day. The ivory skin and the green eyes were just as they had been in Polzeath, but this time there was no amusement about her. No smile. No hint of mercy. Madame Lafayette looked upwards, and the buzzard swooped obediently to hover just above James's head.

"I believe that you have met Olric before, n'est-ce pas?" The mocking words were not spoken as a question, and the petrified children were too shocked to reply. "You have been very brave. You have also been very stupid to get involved in matters you do not understand. I thought you might have learned your lesson after your previous encounter with my men. Especially my darling pet, Olric." At this, she held out her hand, and the buzzard flew across to land gently on it. Upon looking up once more, she fixed the cornered children with a terrifying stare.

James shakily recovered his voice. "Of course. How could we have been so blind not to have worked it out before? Lafayette ... Le Fay. You're Morgana Le Fay, aren't you?"

"So, what if I am, you pathetic little wretch?" she hissed. "Yes, I am Morgana Le Fay, and I have come to receive what should be mine. Long have I waited for this moment, when I shall be only hours from my time of triumph!"

"So it wasn't Hilda after all," groaned Jo, still trying to come to terms with the true identity of Madame Lafayette. "We were convinced she was Morgana Le Fay."

Now a faint smile did begin to curl at the French lady's mouth as she beckoned one of her companions to step forward out of the gloom. Hilda emerged from the crowd to stand expressionless at her side. As yet, not a hand had been laid on any of the children, but they already knew there would be no escape, especially because they felt doubly betrayed by the lady who had befriended them only the previous day.

"It was not my wish for you to be involved," said the elegant Frenchwoman, "and I did warn you to stay away from the caves, did I not? I am, however, extremely grateful that you have brought back to me what I seek."

"I shall never give this sword to you!" snarled James defiantly, and he would have said more if he hadn't been interrupted by Hilda, who seemed to rise in stature as she spoke.

"You stupid children!" Her eyes blazed like fire. "You had no reason to poke your noses into this business. You and that silly little girl with the bucket."

So Lola Mendes had not met with an accident.

"What have you done to her?" asked Jo boldly.

"You will find out soon enough," replied Hilda menacingly, fixing Jo with an icy stare.

OLRIC!

"First, hand over the sword," demanded Morgana, beckoning one of her henchmen forward. But even she was not prepared for the spontaneous courage of Jake, who hurled himself in front of his brother. James ran. It was a hopeless flight because they were surrounded by so many men and moorogs. The ever-present Olric swooped to grip the boy's head in his talons.

Still James ran, screaming as much through fright as pain, with blood drawn by the buzzard's talons trickling down his face. He could not defend himself from the bird, which was beginning to grip the skin around his eyes, because he needed both hands to grasp Excalibur. How James wished he had the power to wield it!

Then the sky erupted in sound.

A huge flock of gulls had arrived in a white cloud of shrieking chaos. Olric was forced to release his grip on James's head, and the boy looked up to see the gulls hurtling into the mass of the crows. Black and white feathers started to flutter downwards, stained with the blood of birds tearing into the flesh of their enemies.

While the aerial battle raged, the beat of hooves could be heard approaching along the clifftop. Somewhere nearby, a trumpet sounded, and war broke out between moorogs, men, and those knights fighting under the banner of Sir Tristram. The warriors of Lyonesse had come to the sword-bearers' aid, determined to prevent Excalibur from falling into enemy hands. All around, there was the sound of metal clashing with metal, the shrieks of the birds, and the yells of fighting men.

Sir Lancelot and several others made straight for James and stood guard around him in order to ensure the sword would not be lost. Amidst the shouting and screeching of the birds, wave upon wave of moorogs threw themselves at the knights, but the thin line of defence held firm as the stinking bodies of their attackers piled up on one another. The grass became a swamp of blood as still more moorogs perished amongst the feathers and mortally wounded birds.

No one had caught Jake when he had thrown himself between James and their foes, and now he was running free amidst the ear-splitting chaos of fighting. No one had noticed him trying to escape from the destruction around him. He found a large rock, lay behind it, and was able to watch the battle unfolding before him.

Morgana Le Fay

The defence around James and Excalibur continued to hold while the fight raged on between knights and men and moorogs, axes clashing with swords. Although outnumbered, the discipline of the knights seemed to be winning the day, as more and more bodies of moorogs littered the field. Meanwhile, feathers fell like snowflakes, and dying birds fell to earth, their battles done.

While looking out from his hiding-place, Jake was relieved to see Jo was not involved in the fighting. His relief turned to horror when he saw she was held captive by a soldier and none other than Morgana Le Fay herself, who remained standing serene amidst the destruction. Jo could sense the woman's fury that her plans had been undone, and Excalibur was still kept from her. She wriggled free and bit the man holding her, kicking him hard on the shin before running away in the direction of Jake. As she ran up the slope from the cliff, Jake heard himself calling her name and urging her on, but hopes were dashed as her freedom was short-lived. One of Morgana's men caught up with her and knocked her to the ground before carrying the limp, unconscious body back to his mistress.

Jake knew that pursuit would be hopeless, so he sank dejectedly back behind the rock. Moments later, he froze in terror, feeling something prod into his back. He awaited the inevitable blow from a moorog's axe. The prodding continued, accompanied by a snuffling sound. He slowly turned to find himself staring into the nostrils of his pony and, standing behind, the reassuring figure of Merlin. The wizard smiled at him, although he could not totally hide his concern over the deadly battle in front of them.

The sky was beginning to clear, and a red glow over the eastern horizon heralded the arrival of dawn. Many birds on both sides had perished, and those which remained were flapping unsteadily away from the carnage. The knights guarding James and Excalibur had nearly repelled all their attackers, and those who had survived were beginning to retreat into the gloom.

Morgana herself and her entourage were now departing the scene, admitting defeat in this battle. The unconscious Jo, however, was still in her hands as a hostage, and she was determined to return in even greater strength the next time she led her army against the Knights of the Round Table.

"The day may be yours, but I shall return. I shall have my way!" she screamed, and her voice became a screech as she turned once more. "Oh yes, I shall have my way!"

Then she was gone.

Merlin carefully placed Jake on his pony, and together, they trotted up to Sir Lancelot and his band of victorious knights. James was still lying face down amongst them, and when he was rolled over, the feathery silk shroud lay a little bloodstained beneath him. His face, however, was a mess. Olric's talons had drawn a lot of blood, but there was widespread relief that his eyes appeared to have survived the vicious onslaught. Sir Lancelot picked up the shroud and unwrapped it to reveal the sword's hilt and scabbard. Everyone gazed at it in awe before he passed it to Merlin.

"It is best that Excalibur is entrusted to a wizard's care and not into the hands of any warrior," he said. He then turned to the boys. "You two did well tonight, and your courage has kept the great sword safe from falling into evil hands." He paused and surveyed the scene. "But where is your sister? Is she all right?"

Jake described how Jo had been held before breaking free and then being felled.

"Is she okay now?" asked James.

"I'm afraid your sister is in the hands of Morgana Le Fay," announced Merlin grimly. "I am sure that she will come to no further harm yet, but she will be held hostage. I have no doubt that the ransom for her return will be Excalibur."

An air of dejection greeted these words, and eventually the silence was broken by Sir Tristram. "We must return to Lyonesse. Gather the wounded. Sound the trumpet, for we have won a great battle this morning. Not a man amongst us has died."

"Not a man, maybe, but we have lost a girl. As Knights of the Round Table, it is our bounden duty to rescue her," added Sir Lancelot as the victorious army descended the cliff, heading out over the waves to the city at bottom of the sea the sea.

Chapter 11

Captivity

"Hello."

Jo was sure she had heard a voice but was not sure it was speaking to her. In fact, she had no idea where she was. All she was certain about was that she had a very sore head, and gradually memories drifted back. She shuddered while thinking about the battle on the clifftop after the hazardous return from Dozmary Pool. She recalled the magical meeting with the Lady of the Lake, the sight of Excalibur and then the rescue at Delphy Bridge. Her heart sank as her mind drifted to the shocking discovery that the beautiful Madame Lafayette was in truth the evil Morgana Le Fay. *I can't believe such a beautiful person could be so wicked!* The ground seemed to be moving slightly, and there was a humming noise somewhere in the distance. She drifted once more into unconsciousness.

"Hello."

This time it was louder, and Jo realised it *was* a voice—and it came from nearby. She tried to move but found she was trussed up like a Christmas turkey, a rope tightly binding her wrists and ankles. *Ouch, my head!* She managed to twist herself round to see where the voice had come from and there, also tied up as a captive, was another girl, whose wide eyes were staring at her.

"Hello." This was the third greeting from the other prisoner, and this time Jo was able to respond.

"Hi, I'm Jo. You're not called Lola, are you?" The other girl nodded. "Lola Mendes?" Another nod. Jo gasped, feeling an enormous sense of relief at realising the missing girl was still alive. "The whole world's been looking for you. Are you all right?" she asked excitedly, forgetting her own pain for a moment.

"About as all right as you, I suppose. I haven't been on this boat for very long, but it's better than the dark dungeon I was in before. That was *really* creepy. It was damp and cold, and it stank!"

"Boat?" That explained why the "ground" was moving; the humming noise must be the engine. Jo was pretty sure she knew this boat, guessing it was the one she'd been on the previous day. "Lola, have you met the owner of this boat?"

"I don't think so. I've only met some of the crew—horrible men, and a mean old cow called Hilda. None of them ever smile. As I say, I was kept in some damp, dark cave for what seemed like days before they brought me over here in a dinghy. That trip was rough, but I couldn't see anything because I was wrapped up in some big, smelly bag that stank of fish. Yuk!"

Jo's mind went back to the night before when they had seen the men carrying the large bundle across the beach to the dinghy. *So it was Lola they were carrying, not treasure!* In the 3Js' haste to go to Dozmary Pool, they had thought little about the bag, and it had not occurred to them that it might have been the missing child who was being taken out of the cave. It also helped to explain why they had been attacked there at the rock pool and why they had seen Hilda lurking at the entrance. The cave had hidden an important secret, and maybe there *was* a tunnel to the farmhouse.

"Lola, did this Hilda visit you in the cave?"

"Yes, she did. Although she's a nasty old witch, she did bring me food and water, and also some clothes. I'd have died without this fleece."

"Hold on, Lola! That's *my* fleece! I've been looking for it everywhere. Hilda must have taken it out of my room and given it to you!"

"Well, thanks, Jo. I must say I'm glad she did. The other clothes must have been yours too."

"I'm glad she took them, Lola. It must've been terrible."

"It was! It was really scary and dark in there, and it seemed as if she didn't come from the beach but from a tunnel leading inland." So there *was* a tunnel—and Jo had a good idea where it led. She told Lola about the farmhouse and her own distrust of Hilda, but her head really hurt now, and she found herself unable to talk anymore. The story seemed too complicated and, as she became delirious, she thought of her brothers and their hopeless plight up on the cliffs. "I'm sorry, Lola, but I need to sleep. Do you know if they brought any other prisoners onto the boat?"

Lola did not need to answer because Jo was already asleep.

James opened his eyes to see the face of Lady Isabelle. There was an ageless wisdom about her beauty. She showed concern for him as she mopped his brow with a soft cloth.

"How is he?" James recognised the voice of Merlin.

"The scars will heal quickly. He is fortunate the bird did not damage his eyes, for his sight might have been lost."

"Fortunate indeed," agreed the wizard. "But it is no accident that James's eyes remained safe. Anyone bearing the scabbard of Excalibur is protected from harm by the Lady's spell. Would that King Arthur had been wearing it at the Battle of Camlann!"

"Did you take the sword from me?" James asked anxiously. The memory of Olric's attack flooded back to him.

"Indeed so," replied Merlin soothingly. "Your courage ensured that Excalibur was shielded from evil hands, and the sword now lies safely under our protection."

Although James was relieved to hear this, there was something about Merlin's manner which filled him with unease. "Is something wrong, Merlin?"

"You need to rest, James. Presently you will be told about all that has happened." So gentle and hypnotic were Isabelle's words that James gratefully sank into oblivion once more, and he did not see the look of concern she directed at Merlin. The wizard stood up and left the room.

Meanwhile, Jake was with Cabhan, who was cleaning and sharpening swords following the battle.

"Unreal! Look at all those swords. I've only seen them in museums before. This is so cool," said Jake.

"Once I have finished with these, I shall make you a sword of your own," promised the craftsman.

"Wow!" said Jake. "Will you really? Can I watch you making it?"

"Of course. Anyone who serves in the army of Lyonesse must have his own sword." At this, Jake felt immensely proud, and he started to dance

OLRIC!

around, imagining that he was slaying moorogs by the score. "I shall need to measure your hands and the length of your arms to make sure it is a perfect size and weight for you."

"Unreal!" replied Jake.

"Good morning, Hilda!" Matty Petherick was in his usual good spirits as he entered the kitchen. His housekeeper smiled while placing his breakfast on the table: two slices of hog's pudding, egg, bacon, mushrooms, and toast. He preferred fried bread, but he had decided a long time ago to pay token regard to healthy living. "Delicious as usual. I shall be away until mid-afternoon, Hilda—some business to attend to in Wadebridge. You'll be all right with the children, I hope?"

"Of course, Mr Petherick. I shall enjoy looking after them." *This arrangement could not be better,* she thought, and she smiled as she brought a pot of tea to the table.

A little later, Matty loaded his clubs into the back of his car and set off down the lane. Business in Wadebridge looked like eighteen holes at St Enodoc. Hilda was delighted that Matty was out of the way. *He will be out for at least four hours,* she thought, and she returned to what she knew to be a deserted farmhouse.

After locking the door behind her, she walked swiftly to the dining room. She pushed up the beak of the carved seagull on the wall and the oak panelling slid aside to reveal the entrance to the passage. She passed through into the tunnel, and the damp, smelly air hit her as she made her way through the cave to the beach before boarding the waiting dinghy, which would take her out to *La Mirabelle*.

When she woke up, Jo felt a good deal better, although her head continued to ache. Lola's eyes were still focused on her, showing delight that she was awake once more.

"Are you okay now, Jo?"

"Yes, I think so. Lola, please tell me what happened when you were taken prisoner on the beach."

"It all happened so suddenly. Mum and Dad were dozing after lunch on the beach, so I decided to sneak away and explore the next bay behind the rocks. I remember finding a fascinating pool, and I was just watching some fish darting to and fro amongst the seaweed when I looked up and saw the entrance to a big cave."

"Yes, I know that cave. I was attacked by a bird in the same place."

"I just couldn't resist having a look, so I ran over to it. There was a horrid smell in there. I went in farther, and there was a huge, slimy monster. That was why it stank. When it stood up, I'd never been so scared in my life. It had one eye and waved an axe at me."

"Moorog. Must have been."

"Moorog? Have you seen one then?" Before Jo could reply, Lola went on. "I turned to run back to the pool when something hit me. Next thing I knew, I was tied up in the darkness, all alone until that Hilda woman brought me some food."

"I don't suppose it was tuna bake?"

"Why, yes, it was. How do you know?"

"It's what Hilda cooked for us when we arrived at Uncle Matty's farm. She must have brought you the leftovers through the tunnel."

"I hate tuna. Who's Uncle Matty?"

Jo explained a little of her family history and described how they had heard Matty's voice on the radio as they travelled through Devon. "I'm so glad you're safe, Lola. Everyone thought you'd drowned."

"Safe? Do you call this safe?"

"We'll get out of here somehow." Jo did not feel as confident as she sounded, knowing a little more about the ruthlessness of their captors. "If they were going to kill us, they'd have done it by now."

"Were they asking for a ransom?"

"No. That's why everyone still thinks you were washed out to sea. James had a theory—he's always having theories—that you must have been abducted, but the police couldn't find any more evidence of it." She described how her brother had based his idea on the positioning of the shoes.

"He must be a clever boy, your brother."

"He thinks so. He can get on my nerves big time."

"I wish I had a brother."

OLRIC!

"You wouldn't say that if you did. Brothers are pains!" As she said this, Jo felt guilty and wondered if James and Jake were all right.

James sat in the great hall with Sir Tristram on his right, Merlin on his left, and opposite them Sir Lancelot, Lady Isabelle, and Jake.

Sir Tristram spoke first. "As I said earlier, you boys acted very bravely to bring Excalibur back to us. To have surrendered the great sword to Morgana would have been disastrous."

"I don't think we'd have managed it if Jake hadn't thrown himself in front of me on the cliff," said James. "That gave me time to run."

Jake felt remarkably proud of himself, especially when he realised all eyes were looking at him. "Oh, it was nothing, really. Anyone else would have done the same," he said almost casually. Then he felt guilty for wallowing in his own pride. "I just wish I had saved Jo. What will they do to her?" No one had an answer to this question, and there was a pause while they grimly contemplated her capture.

"At least the moorogs did not take her. There has to be a good chance we shall find her safe," said Sir Lancelot.

"They will not harm her while we have the sword," said Merlin. "Morgana may yet use her to bargain." They all fell silent, knowing Jo's fate was no longer in their hands.

Presently, the boys were asked to give an account of their journey to Dozmary Pool and their dealings with the Lady of the Lake. They took it in turns to give an accurate description of their ride across the moor and the spectacular lighting effects when the Lady herself had first appeared and then had surfaced again, bearing Excalibur.

"It was just amazing, wasn't it, Jake?" said James. "I just can't begin to describe how incredible it was when that shining blade came up through the water!"

"What did the Lady say?" asked Merlin. Both James and Jake found it difficult to remember her exact words, although they did remember she'd spoken in a riddle before she had left them.

"Seek the something on the tor," started Jake.

"No, seek the something as before."

"Seek the *eagle* as before," Jake said with authority, and he was joined in unison by James, "when moonlight sweeps across the tor."

"There will be pointed," continued James.

"As Joseph anointed," added Jake.

"The chalice as told in folklore," they almost shouted triumphantly. They were asked to repeat the riddle, and this they willingly did:

> "Seek the eagle as before
> When moonlight sweeps across the tor.
> There will be pointed,
> As Joseph anointed,
> The chalice as told in folklore."

"What do you make of these words, Merlin?" asked Sir Lancelot.

The wizard paused for a long time before he spoke. "The eagle I do not yet understand, for it is a bird that has not been seen in these parts for centuries. The tor must be the hill overlooking Avalon."

"Avalon?" interrupted Jake. All eyes looked impatiently at the boy because this was not the first time his voice had disturbed their thoughts.

Surprisingly, James joined his brother in diverting Merlin from his thoughts. "Yes, the Lady mentioned Avalon."

"What did the Lady say?" asked Sir Lancelot earnestly.

"The king sleeps in Avalon's vale, or something like that."

"It is as I thought," said Merlin. "The tor must be that at Avalon. She said no more about eagles?"

"Absolutely certain," confirmed James. "It was only the mention of the king sleeping in Avalon's vale."

"Why was the name Joseph also mentioned?" queried Sir Lancelot.

"Probably Joseph of Arimethea. He is said to have brought the Holy Grail, containing the blood of Christ, to England," said Merlin.

"That would be the chalice, then?" asked Sir Tristram.

"Most likely, although I am surprised the Lady of the Lake is aware of the Grail, let alone that it is at Avalon."

"Merlin, you've lost us. Please can you explain who or what is Avalon?" asked James.

"It is a place, which is known these days as Glastonbury."

"Glastonbury?" chirped Jake excitedly. "That's where there's a festival, isn't it, James?"

Merlin continued before James could reply. "Once it was an island, and men could sail there from distant lands. The Tor is a mystical hill steeped in legends, and at its foot lies the ruins of an abbey that dominates the sacred ground of Avalon itself. There is a thorn tree, planted by Joseph, which flowers every year on Christmas Day. For many it remains the holiest Christian site in Britain, and this is why we must go there with Excalibur to awaken the Great King himself. He lies, as the Lady says, in Avalon's Vale."

"Then we march to Avalon," announced Sir Lancelot. "There we shall seek to awaken the Great King. With the mighty power of Excalibur and the blessing of the Lady of the Lake, we shall summon the forces to reunite the Round Table itself!"

As he finished speaking, the Great Hall of Lyonesse echoed to the cheering of all who stood there.

"Lola, can you swim?"

"Yes, I belong to a swimming club at home. I've got loads of badges. Why?"

"I think I can guess where we are. If I'm right, we could get ashore, as long as the currents aren't too strong."

"Great idea, Jo, but haven't you forgotten something? We're tied up, the door's probably locked, and this boat has those horrid men on board. We'd never reach the deck."

"Surely it's worth a try, Lola. After all, they aren't likely to let us go, so we have to find a way to escape."

"Okay, game on. If we can wriggle closer, we may be able to untie each other's knots." Both the girls hauled themselves, amidst a lot of giggling, closer to each other and found they could touch hands by lying back to back.

"If only I had a knife," muttered Jo.

"Thank goodness you haven't. You'd most likely cut my wrists, and there'd be blood everywhere!"

Captivity

After several minutes, the girls had made things even more difficult for themselves. They had both found ends of rope and managed to untie the knots, but in doing so, they had only succeeded in somehow tying themselves together! In spite of their grim situation, this caused a further outbreak of giggles. Finally pulling themselves together, they decided that only one of them should work at the rope, and Lola set to while Jo lay wondering how far they would have to swim to safety.

Presently, Lola gave a whoop of triumph, and Jo found she was able to move her hands once more. She knelt over Lola's back and soon succeeded in releasing her.

"Brilliant!" said Lola. "What now?" The sound of voices outside the cabin caused them to freeze, not knowing what to do.

"Quick! Lie down again and pretend we're still tied up!" They frantically lay back down with their hands behind their backs as the door handle turned, and they hoped their visitor would assume they were still bound.

It was Loveless, the man who had been so brutal to Jo on the beach. She shivered upon remembering their previous encounter, hoping he was not going to touch her. He came towards her and stared viciously at her face, causing her to turn away.

"There is no one to rescue you now, no horses from the sea this time." He laughed, pulling her head round so he could make a mocking, ugly face at her before he left, closing the door behind him and shouting something in a foreign language, presumably informing someone that the prisoners were securely tied up. Jo shook but was determined not to let Lola see how scared she was.

"I felt like spitting in his face!"

"Glad you didn't, but I can't say I blame you. Anyway, come on, Jo. Let's untie our legs. I looked past that horrible man and could see there's a passage leading to steps. They must go up to the deck. The best thing is I don't think there's a lock on the door, and even if there is, I'm sure he didn't turn a key."

"I can't believe it isn't locked."

"One way to find out!"

Moments later, the girls tiptoed to the door, which was not locked, as Lola had thought. It opened quietly when Jo turned the handle. The passage was dimly lit, and the steps were a mere ten metres away. There

OLRIC!

was, however, a cabin beyond the steps, and they could hear angry voices coming from it. They looked at one another, and without a further word, they moved gingerly forward. As they reached the steps, a figure moved into the doorway in front of them. It was Madame Lafayette, but luckily she had her back to them. They were about to move onto the first step when a second person appeared in the cabin. This one was opposite the Frenchwoman, and he had a clear view down the passage.

He was evidently agitated, and the two were arguing. He looked like an elderly professor dressed in a dirty white lab coat, and the fugitives barely dared to breathe because he appeared to be looking straight at them. Girls on the run were clearly not on his mind, however, and he continued to argue in a raised voice.

"Let's go," whispered Lola. "He hasn't noticed us, and with a bit of luck, he's short-sighted." Whether or not Professor Egbert Head could see the girls proceeding up the steps was immaterial, because fleeing captives were of no significance to him.

The steps led up to the main deck on *La Mirabelle*. *This must be the crew's private area*, thought Jo, recalling they had not been invited into that part of the yacht on the previous day's visit. *I can see now why they wouldn't have let us get anywhere near here.* They carefully made their way along the passage towards the door which they hoped would give them access to the outside—and the chance to jump overboard without being seen.

They had reached the door and quietly they pushed it open. They stared outside, looking carefully around them. *Daylight!* A few more steps, and they could see the shore. The yacht floated at anchor in much the same position as when Jo had last seen her, about a hundred metres from the beach. It was such a short distance to freedom despite the treacherous strong currents around Pentire. Jo, remembering her tour of *La Mirabelle*, recognised this as the bridge deck. There were more steps leading down to the lower deck, from which they would have to throw themselves into the sea. There didn't seem to be anyone about, so step by cautious step, they warily descended towards freedom.

Upon reaching the bottom, they turned to their left, full of anticipation and excitement. However, their spirits sank when they saw someone coming round the corner and blocking their way to freedom. It was Hilda. Her face looked like a cruel mask while staring at the girls. She was not alone.

Chapter 12

Despair

There was no escape. Even if they had managed to get past Hilda, Leatherjacketman was standing behind her. They turned round and saw their way was blocked by the threatening presence of Loveless. Even if they had succeeded in jumping overboard, they would never have reached Polzeath alive. These villains could never allow Lola to tell the truth about her disappearance, and the capture of Jo would take a lot of explaining too. In any case, the ability to swim half a mile in a leisure centre pool was no guarantee a child could cover a hundred metres in tidal currents off the Cornish coast.

Hilda stepped towards them and said, "Your stupid uncle is not at home, and you are not going to leave this yacht. Any chance that you might have been released is lost now. Take them back below, Loveless, and this time make sure that they cannot escape."

They were led back to their cell, where the two men tied them up tighter than before, and this time they were gagged as well. All was now lost, and nothing could be heard above the sound of two girls sobbing helplessly in their despair until they drifted into sleep.

When Jo awoke, she was aware of someone else in the cabin. She opened her swollen eyes and saw the tall figure of Morgana Le Fay, alias Madame Lafayette, standing before her. Jo looked defiantly up at her eyes, which glinted cruelly as she stared back at her. She said nothing, but the silence struck fear into Jo's mind, her defiance already being transformed into submission.

OLRIC!

Eventually, Morgana spoke. "Did I not make it absolutely clear you should not interfere with my business? First we have to remove this other prying child before she discovers anything in the cave, and then you and your foolish brothers go and upset everything! You will be sorry to hear they are also in trouble." She beckoned Hilda, who had entered behind her, to release the gag from Jo's mouth.

"Where are they?" Jo gasped as she tried to move farther away from the threatening Frenchwoman

"It is of no matter. You may, however, be able to help them." Seeing Jo was interested in her words, she continued. "You visited a lake on the moor and brought something back with you. What was it, Jo?"

"Don't tell her!" pleaded Lola, who had also had her gag removed. Jo had not yet told her about their errand to Dozmary Pool, but her companion could see she was being goaded into giving away precious information. Jo remained silent and tried to stare back with renewed defiance into the eyes of her inquisitor. There was a pause.

Morgana looked hard at the courageous girl, cowering in front of her. "Do not waste any of my time. I know about the sword."

Jo wondered why she was asking the question if she knew the answer. *And she thinks* I'm *wasting time!*

"I also know who gave you the sword. What you don't understand is that it belongs to me. It would be in my possession but for the scheming sorcery of Merlin. No matter now." Morgana drew herself up to her full height and snarled venomously. "What did the Lady say to you?"

"I don't remember."

"Don't, or won't?" The green eyes pierced through Jo's defences, and Jo looked away. "Look at me!" Jo reluctantly brought her eyes back to face the hypnotic glare. "That's better! Did she say something about a king?" Silence. "Very well, we shall have to prompt your memory. Hilda, take the other child out of here. Kill her!"

Lola gasped in fright as Hilda advanced and roughly bundled her out into the passage, the door closing firmly behind them.

"Well?"

Jo could hear Lola's screams. *I can't let my friend die for this.* So much had happened over the previous three days. Her parents had innocently left them to the mercy of Uncle Matty's cruel and wicked housekeeper.

Despair

Now she had lost both her brothers as well. As the threatening figure of Morgana Le Fay loomed before her, she thought of Lola being needlessly tortured and put to death.

"Wait! I am beginning to remember."

"I thought you might. Go on. What did the Lady say about the king?" Morgana's green eyes continued to bore into Jo's frightened face, staring at her with murderous intent.

Those eyes! she thought, mesmerized. Then she pleaded, "First, let Lola go."

Morgana's eyes flashed even more brightly, now with a strong tint of red to match her hair. Jo looked back at her in horrified fascination. Wisps of smoke floated from her nostrils. In a split second, Morgana's hand moved fast, slapping Jo hard across the face and reducing the girl to tears of pain and terror.

"Don't you dare to give me orders, you insolent child! Tell me exactly what she said."

Screams could still be heard along the passage. Hilda came back into the cabin and quietly closed the door behind her. Lola was now at the mercy of the cruel Loveless and his friends.

"Avalon. The king sleeps in Avalon's something. I'm sorry, I really can't remember anything else." Another piercing stare. "Except I do remember she did talk about a tor or something, and then she mentioned something like palace."

"Palace?"

"No, it might have been chalice."

"That is more likely. Enough. Hilda, fetch the other child. She can be spared for now, if it is not already too late," Morgana said almost casually.

Morgana's appearance had changed back to the image of Madame Lafayette. She almost seemed to smile as she left the cabin, heading for the professor's laboratory a few paces along the passage. The information Jo had supplied was all that was needed to finalise preparations for the comet's descent.

Jo tried to open the door, but it was locked this time, so she sat down and cried at the hopelessness of the situation. A few moments later, the door was opened once more, and her spirits rose at the sight of Lola being led back in.

OLRIC!

Lola's eyes were red and swollen, and she was shaking with fear, but at least she was alive! Both the girls were tied up again, although they were not gagged this time, and when the door was locked once more, they were left alone to comfort one another.

In Whitehall, the government was still no wiser about the riddle that had been sent. Paul had arranged increased security around each royal prince. The Prince of Wales was due to attend a charity concert at the Principality Stadium, Cardiff, that evening. Because this was "in the west", there was lengthy discussion over whether it should be cancelled. Government policy, however, did not allow for giving in to terrorists, so the sell-out event would go ahead as planned. There would, however, be a massive police presence.

The reference to Rangoma's Comet had to be a hoax because it had never been heard of. Leading astronomers around the world had been consulted, but not one had suggested any likelihood of a comet or meteor entering Earth's atmosphere. This was of considerable comfort. If there was no comet to "light the sky", perhaps there would be no "explosions in the west" after all.

Then a further riddle in rhyming couplets was received by the BBC, designed to cause even greater concern to the government and the British people. Nevertheless, the message was withheld from the public for fear of causing mass hysteria.

> Bombs are trained to do their worst;
> Second city will be the first.
> Then will follow a southern town,
> Home to child who strayed to drown.
> One whose loss is mourned out west,
> Paddling away from family nest.

Bombs! England's second city was Birmingham. It was a huge target: large crowds would gather at the shopping centres, and also at the NEC and NIA. Then there was New Street Station, the airport, famous football grounds, and Edgbaston, which was currently host to a cricket test match

Despair

between England and Australia. An explosion at any of these venues would cause massive loss of life. Although security checks had already been organised, it would be very hard to guard against suicide bombers, and the word *trained* gave a clear hint this would be the chosen method to cause maximum destruction.

The second bomb worried Paul personally. Surely it had to refer to the missing child, Lola Mendes, whose home town was Reading. What would a terrorist organisation have to do with such an individual tragedy? He dismissed the possibility of any link between Polzeath and these threats. Colleagues in the cabinet would doubt his professional judgement if he allowed his thoughts to drift to his family holiday. Even so, he was about to call Penmarrett Farm to speak to Matty when his PA came in to summon him to an urgent cabinet meeting.

With a sigh, the minister for defence gathered up his files and left the office. The telephone call would have to wait.

They had only known each other for a few hours, but the two captive girls had already become close friends, and they passed their time together talking about themselves and their families. Because her companion had already been involved to the point of death, Jo felt it important to let Lola know the full story.

It had all started with the news of Lola's disappearance and the family's arrival at Penmarrett, where they had first met the evil Hilda. Then there were the two discoveries that made up the mysterious bell, the involvement of the birds, and the chance meeting with Madame Lafayette, who had so impressed Uncle Matty. Lola found the account of the journey to Lyonesse too fantastic to believe, especially when she heard the description of riding over the moor to meet the Lady of the Lake. It all became more real, however, when it led to the clifftop battle and Jo's capture.

"Incredible!" she uttered when her friend had finished. "Those moorogs are disgusting, aren't they? My story's much less exciting than yours, Jo."

"But you were all alone, weren't you, Lola? At least I had my brothers with me." Saying this reminded her that James and Jake were no longer with her. "I do hope they're all right."

OLRIC!

She did not have long to think about her brothers. At that moment, the cabin door opened, and there in front of them stood Hilda. She closed the door behind her, and a strange smile of wicked intent spread across her face as she produced from her apron pocket a long-bladed vegetable knife.

Cabhan came racing up to Jake as he sat patiently on his pony amidst the entire fighting force of Lyonesse.

"Here is your sword, Jake. Treat it well, and it will look after you. I have also made one for James. Where is he?"

Jake pointed away to his left, where his brother was talking to Merlin, and then looked down at his sword. He pulled it proudly from its scabbard. The blade was sharp, and the metal glinted as he held it by its hilt. Jake saw his name had been carefully inscribed on the blade amongst shells and waves and sea creatures. He looked up once more to see Cabhan coming back towards him.

"Do you like it, Jake?"

"Like it? It's the coolest thing I've ever seen! Thank you, Cabhan!"

"Good, but remember it is not just an ornament. It is for your protection, a weapon for the slaughter of your enemies. Ah, here is James. I am pleased that I shall see you both put your swords to good use, for I am to accompany you to Avalon."

Loud cheers erupted around them as Sir Tristram of Tintagel Castle and Lyonesse appeared at the head of his army. He turned to exhort his men before leading them up from the depths once more, this time in the hope of awakening an even greater leader, King Arthur himself, to bring peace back to the troubled world.

The cabinet meeting had taken up most of the day, and Paul inwardly felt the strain of his office. Many items had been on the agenda in addition to the anonymous threats, but all had been connected to the security of the country. The prime minister and all his colleagues had shared his concerns for the Prince of Wales, although they had considered the latest bomb threat to be a hoax. It was ridiculous, it had been pointed out, to suppose

Despair

a terrorist organisation would show any interest in a child's disappearance from a Cornish beach.

Maybe it was his own connection with Polzeath making the words continue to spin round in his head as he returned home that evening, but whatever the reason, he would see what Sarah made of the riddles.

"Yes, it has to be a hoax, Paul," she agreed after reading the scripted verse. "But who would be so sick as to make a joke out of little Lola's disappearance? There are always Cornish nationalists eager to form a republic, but bombs of mass destruction and celebrating tragedy is not their style."

"Have you been in touch with the children?"

"No. I agreed with Uncle Matty that I wouldn't ring them. They'll be having a great time, and speaking over the phone might make them homesick."

"I couldn't agree with you more. They'll be having a super time without us around. I only hope they don't drive poor Hilda up the wall!"

"Well, if Uncle Matty finds he needs some peace and quiet, he can always put them on the train." Sarah laughed, but then her expression suddenly changed. "Could I have another look at that riddle, please?"

"Your crossword-solving brain getting to work?" He passed the paper to her.

"'Bombs are trained to do their worst.' You were thinking of suicide bombers being trained, weren't you?"

"Yes, or possibly the bombs being aimed at their targets from a distance."

"It could be so much simpler, Paul. Bombs trained. Bombs transported by train?"

The minister for defence leapt into action. Of course that would make sense. Where these bombs came from was not of immediate concern, but their destinations were clear if Sarah's theory was correct. Within minutes, security services and bomb disposal teams were on the way to both Reading Station and Birmingham New Street.

All Paul could do now was to sit and wait.

OLRIC!

Merlin's spell ensured no human eye could see the army from Lyonesse secretly riding over the waves that night to climb the cliff and bear northeastwards towards Glastonbury. Jake and James once again clung to their trusted ponies. At the same time, Hilda stood outside Penmarrett House, urgently giving final instructions to Loveless and Growles before they proceeded to load the trunks, packed with explosives, into the van awaiting them.

It had been quite a challenge to unload them from *La Mirabelle* into the waiting dinghies and then ferry them on the incoming tide to the cave. From there, it had been a case of carrying them one by one through the tunnel to the farmhouse dining room. Hilda had made sure Matty was out. He had been invited to dinner on board *La Mirabelle*. Everything had depended upon Penmarrett being deserted this evening. Matty Petherick was certain to accept an invitation from the delightful Madame Lafayette as long as he could rely on Hilda to see to the children. She thought she had seen to them rather well!

The van turned left out of the farm gate and headed for Bodmin Parkway station. When they got there, both Loveless and Growles waited patiently for their train. Loveless was bound for Birmingham, but his companion would change at Exeter for the Paddington train, which would stop at Reading. Growles was already familiar with this line. He had tracked down that suitcase near Liskeard in the hope of finding the bell so keenly sought by his employer.

Meanwhile, Hilda removed any evidence of two heavy trunks being dragged through the house before retiring to her room. Mr Petherick would expect her to be in the house when he returned from his dinner engagement. Half an hour later, she heard the taxi come up the drive, and she went down to greet her employer at the front door.

"Did you have a nice evening, Mr Petherick?"

"Absolutely splendid, thank you. Madame Lafayette has an excellent chef, and I'd swear the mackerel had only been out of the sea for a few minutes before it appeared on the plate."

This might be truer than he realises, thought Hilda, because the crew could have caught some fish on their way back from leaving the trunks in the cave!

"Are the children all right?" Matty asked.

"Of course, Mr Petherick. They have had an interesting day and are tired. I am sure that they will tell you all about it in the morning."

"Splendid!" said Matty as he sat back to enjoy the generous glass of brandy Hilda had placed before him.

"Goodnight, Mr Petherick," said Hilda as she left the room. Later, she would secretly make her way back to the shore, where the dinghy would be waiting. She had something else to attend to on *La Mirabelle*.

Chapter 13

The Approach to Avalon

Morgana Le Fay was in good spirits, considering she had not managed to get her hands on Excalibur. It was true she still had to make sure the Round Table could not reform. She was also mindful that the magic of Merlin, as well as that of the Lady of the Lake, had yet to be overcome. Still, all else was in place to guarantee her inevitable triumph.

Her professor seemed to have succeeded in controlling the meteor, now programmed for the destruction of Avalon, and her bombs were on their way to create havoc in the heart of the country. The little girls had both proved to be a nuisance, but neither held any useful purpose for her now. It did not matter whether they lived or didn't. If Hilda had not already killed them, they would soon be dead, and she had found it amusing to listen to that silly old farmer talking proudly about the children while she had entertained him for dinner. It had been tempting to do away with him as well, but his suffering would be all the greater when he discovered the trust of his sister had been so misplaced.

She paid one more visit to Egbert Head to check that his work was still going according to plan. After deciding it was, she went up to the bridge. The dinghy which had taken Matty Petherick back ashore had now returned with Hilda, and Morgana gave the command to proceed at full throttle into the Bristol Channel towards the Somerset coast. While the launch accelerated away past Pentire Point, Morgana made her way to the luxurious cabin below decks.

The Approach to Avalon

Loveless looked at his watch and smiled complacently as the train rolled into Exeter St David's dead on time. He assisted Growles onto the platform with his trunk, and the two men wished each other good luck before they continued on their separate ways. No one would have an inkling these two men were terrorists with no regard for human life, nor that they were intent on blowing up two major stations.

Loveless's train continued on its way. As it pulled out of Taunton, he was pleased to receive a text message from Growles, informing him that his connection to Reading on the Paddington train had also departed on time. Both men were now approximately two hours from their destinations. Loveless would contact the professor again after leaving the train at Cheltenham so that Egbert Head would know when to detonate the bombs via remote control.

Not very far away, only half a mile inland, Excalibur was being borne across Exmoor by the devoted and determined band of knights. It was an impressive sight, with horses and ponies barely touching the ground as they sped over the rolling hills. This was even more exhilarating than the ride to Dozmary Pool. Now the boys were travelling in a large cavalry. On every side, there were knights in gleaming armour, and many were carrying colourful banners. These warriors of ancient times had long lived for this moment as they rode once more in pursuit of glory.

Sir Lancelot du Lac looked magnificent, leading his closest band of knights who had shared with him the honour of sitting at the Round Table. Whilst waiting in Lyonesse, Cabhan had told many tales of the exploits of such legendary heroes as Sir Gawain, Sir Bors, Sir Tristram, and Sir Percival. While riding now amongst these gallant men, it was easy to imagine how they had earned their reputations in the glorious days of old.

Sergeant Cruickshank had seen service in Iraq and Afghanistan, so a stint of duty at Birmingham New Street Station might have seemed less than exciting, yet he was the model professional, a soldier trained to do his duty in whatever capacity the job demanded. As a member of the bomb

OLRIC!

disposal unit, he was accustomed to treating each moment as if it was his last, so his sharp eyes and attention to detail never missed anything suspicious.

The train from Penzance had just arrived, and a lot of passengers made their way out along the platform. None of them was wearing any bulky clothing, so a suicide bomber was unlikely to be in this group. While his men carried out a meticulous search of baggage, he looked up the next train due to arrive. This was from London Euston and seemed a much more likely target.

Suddenly, his pager bleeped. An abandoned trunk had been found on the Penzance train.

The entire station was evacuated in minutes. Roads were cleared around it, causing gridlock in the city centre. This was when Cruickshank's training came into its own. Once he had been informed where the trunk was, he crept stealthily onto the train with a cable. This he would connect to the trunk and move away in order to detonate a controlled explosion. If he made any error, the chances were that his death would be instantaneous, and few traces of his body would ever be found amongst the ensuing debris.

As he connected the cable to the trunk, Sergeant Cruickshank talked to himself. He always did this in order to calm his nerves. Never before, however, had he known his target to reply, so he could not believe his ears when he heard a child's voice.

"Love a duck," he said out loud. "I must be going mad. I'm sure I heard a voice in there."

"Please let me out!"

"Blimey! There *is* someone in there, or else I really *am* going mad." He opened the trunk. The other members of his unit couldn't believe their eyes when they saw what he was doing. Their shock was about to be as great as his because lying and staring up at him from a padded bed, was a young, fair-haired girl shielding her eyes from the light.

"Is this Birmingham or Reading?" she enquired.

When Hilda had produced the knife, Jo and Lola had feared the worst. Uncle Matty's housekeeper had put her fingers to her lips and hurriedly whispered she had come to help them escape, using the knife to cut through the tough ropes binding the two girls together. She urgently explained what they needed to do.

"In the next cabin, there are two trunks, each with a bomb inside. Later tonight, these trunks will be taken ashore and put on a train. One is for Birmingham, and the other is for Reading."

Lola gasped. "Reading? That's where I live!"

"Each bomb is fitted with a detonator," continued Hilda, "so the explosion can be set off by a mobile phone."

"That's awful!" exclaimed Jo. "Why would she do this?"

"There is no time to explain now. But you must trust me. We have to take the bombs out of the trunks, and you are to get into them. Stay in the trunks, and you may have a chance to escape—as long as her men do not realise what has happened."

"I don't like the sound of this one bit," said Lola.

"It will not be comfortable, but the alternative is certain death. Madame has no mercy, and you are of no use to her now." The girls stared back at Hilda and nodded, paling as the impact of her words struck them. "Come, we need to move those bombs."

They crept out into the passage, and Hilda led them into the next cabin, where two large metal trunks lay on the floor. They swiftly set to work, lifting each bomb carefully out of the trunks and placing them into large sail bags.

"Hilda," asked Jo shakily, "how are we going to breathe? And why are you helping us?"

"You will notice that there are vents in each trunk. I can only hope they will let in enough air for you to breathe. Do not ask why I am doing this. I simply want you to realise I am not really one of them, even if you have thought so up until now."

"Are you really a spy, then?" asked Jo.

"In a way, I suppose," replied Hilda.

"You must be a double agent," concluded Lola.

"No, I am not that. One day, maybe I explain. I hope that day will come soon, but now we must hide these bombs."

The girls helped Hilda to take the two bags, now heavy with a bomb in each one, back to their cabins. She would try to make them appear like

OLRIC!

the dead bodies of the two girls before zipping them up. Then they tiptoed back to climb into the trunks. Luckily, there was a lot of padding in them to stop the bombs from rolling around, so there would at least be some comfort for the girls on their journeys. Hilda assured them they should not have long to wait as she prepared to fasten the lids of the trunks.

Lola felt a fresh level of fear, verging on panic. "How do we know we can trust you?" she asked, wide-eyed with fear.

"You cannot know, but let me say this. It would be easy to have killed you both, if I had not wanted to save you. Now, I must leave before we are discovered. Goodbye, and good luck!" After saying this, she made sure both trunks were closed and fastened before she left the cabin.

Shortly afterwards, they heard the door opening and the voices of men in the cabin. Each girl felt a jolt as the trunks were lifted and carried up to the deck. Lola had to suppress a fit of giggles while listening to the curses of the men. Although she didn't understand the language, she guessed they must have been very rude words. Both trunks were gently lowered into the waiting dinghies, and the girls could feel the motion of the water lapping around them.

Orders were being given to the crew. The dinghies were cast off, and the girls heard the movement of oars above the lapping water as they were ferried ashore. Little was said until the dinghies reached the beach and came to a shuddering halt. The trunks were lifted and carried clumsily across the sand. *I bet we're going to Penmarrett through the cave and tunnel,* thought Jo. She was right. The trunks were carried into the dining room and out through the front door. From there, they were loaded into a waiting van and driven to the station, while Uncle Matty had still been dining aboard the yacht.

Following the surprise discovery of Jo, the bomb disposal team at Reading had been informed about the second trunk, and as Lola was carried out to the waiting ambulance, there was jubilation amongst those who had found her. For the time being, the news was a closely guarded secret. The girls had been placed in a secret location along with their relieved and delighted parents. This was partly for security and also to keep them away from the media.

Their secluded hotel was set in its own grounds, close to a village in rural Somerset. The girls themselves had become inseparable friends, and they insisted on sharing a room, where they could talk about their imprisonment, the surprise release by Hilda of all people, and their less than comfortable journeys to freedom. In due course, a doctor was coming to give them both a thorough medical check following their ordeals.

George Varley had spent a long day at the wheel of his combine harvester. If the weather was dry and the corn was ripe, no time would be wasted in ensuring the barley was cut, so he was accustomed to driving throughout the night if need be. He stopped for a brief rest and got out of his cab to stretch his legs and have a chicken and cucumber sandwich. He looked out over the Devon coast towards the lights on Lundy Island.

He had taken a second bite of his sandwich when he was suddenly amazed to see a brilliant glow, like a red fireball, light up the sea a mile or so offshore. As he stared at it, a loud explosion shook the air, and a huge pillar of water shot up from the same spot. He continued to stare, open-mouthed, upon seeing huge waves rise and roll towards the shore before the red glow began to die.

"Holy cucumbers!" he said, wondering if he was in a fit state to get back in the cab.

Sir Tristram halted at the head of the army, and his horse stood motionless. Merlin appeared at his side and beckoned James and Jake towards them. He pointed to a distant shape rising in the dim light out of the plain ahead, a perfectly shaped hill like a rounded sandcastle with a tower at its summit.

"Avalon, the Isle of the Dead," he announced. "That is the tor of legend, as spoken by the Lady when she met you at Dozmary. We must proceed with caution. I fear we are not alone this night."

They advanced in the shadowy gloom, treading carefully along a wide ridge flanked on both sides by marshes. The army moved with solemn

OLRIC!

purpose, eyes peeled for any movement and ears trained for sounds that might alert them to danger.

When the sound came, it still caused the horses and ponies to rear and the men to stop in their tracks: a loud, blood-curdling shriek broke the stillness to the right, a terrifying wail that could not possibly have come through human lips. Just as they were restoring their composure, a second and even more frightening scream came from the left, and the boys began to tremble.

"Keep on the ridge!" shouted Merlin. "These sounds are merely sorcery to strike fear into us! As long as we do not stray into the marshes, we shall be safe." In response to these words, the knights gave a loud, defiant cheer and continued to advance with self-belief restored.

"James." The voice was a deep whisper, and he did not realise that he alone had heard it. "James, come to me, and great will be your reward." He looked up, and there beside him was a snow-white horse. On its back rode a lady, also dressed in white, whose face seemed to be drained of blood, although it still appeared to be smiling at him. She stretched out her hand, and he felt himself respond to her lead, reaching out to touch it.

"Who are you?" asked James shakily.

"My name is Rhiannon. Come, James, follow me." As he obediently went after the white horse, he did not realise he was straying from the ridge. Neither did he hear his brother urgently calling out his name. Cabhan noticed what was happening and rode swiftly to James's side, but he could not make himself heard. He grasped the pony's mane, but still James advanced towards the edge of the ridge in a hypnotic trance, pulling Cabhan along with him

"Taramar loc guenneth!" The voice was that of Merlin and James's pony veered back towards the marching army. There was a piercing shriek from where it had been heading and soon James was back next to Jake, his eyes staring without sight before him.

"He has been bewitched," announced Merlin, who then addressed James in a strange tongue. "Bi cwilteth si cruanna, ty mwn fo stanled." There was another scream, but this time it was James. His head fell forward, chin resting on his chest. Merlin reached out and touched him. Suddenly James woke from his trance and was able to describe what he had seen. Merlin listened gravely before he replied, "Rhiannon is a keeper of the tor, home to the goddess of the Underworld. There are nine keepers in all, and their presence on the marshes will make our quest more difficult."

"Do you think they serve Morgana?" enquired Sir Lancelot.

"I think not," replied the wizard. "They serve only their goddess, and she will answer to no one. If she is aware of our quest, she will not willingly release the Great King, and she will be eager to claim Excalibur from us."

Merlin had no sooner finished speaking than the night air was filled with the sound of baying hounds ahead. Out of the shadows emerged a pack of white dogs, which snarled at the advancing men, red eyes staring with vicious intent and muzzles drooling in anticipation. Behind them, shrouded in a thin mist and holding a long, pointed spear at his side, stood a tall figure that was human in body but with the head of a stag.

"The Hunter!" gasped Merlin. "Another who serves the goddess!"

The Hunter raised his spear and pointed at the fighting force of Lyonesse. He issued a command to his hounds, who responded by charging ferociously towards the surprised army.

The leading dog took off and flew with bared teeth at Sir Lancelot, only to be felled by his shield. The rest of the pack went on. Jake was terrified. He drew his sword and held it out in front of him. He shut his eyes and hoped these beasts did not attack. As he did so, his blade moved in his tight grasp, and he looked down to see a dead hound at his feet. It had been slit open from its neck to its stomach, its entrails bleeding into the soil around it. Then he passed out.

The doctor stepped out of the lift on the third floor and turned left along the corridor. It was clear which room to head for, since there was yet another security guard standing outside it. The guard glanced at the ID card and opened the door, informing the girls the doctor had arrived, before closing it once more.

"Hi," said Lola, welcoming the doctor before she looked up to see who it was. Her heart went to stone. Standing in front of her with a triumphant leer was no doctor, but Morgana Le Fay! Jo tried to scream but found that she could not make any sound. The "doctor" had cast a spell of silence.

The girls left the room, held tightly by their captor. They walked past the guard, who was now asleep, and left the hotel. They passed other security men who had come under Morgana's spell before being pushed into a waiting blue van. With hope ebbing away, Jo recognised the driver as McCulloch, one of the villains at the cave.

"I am sure you would like to see your brothers again, Jo," said Morgan as the van pulled onto the main road. "I am glad that you did not die on my boat, because you can both be of more use to me alive."

"How did you know where we were?" asked Lola.

Morgana said nothing, but both girls followed her gaze. Perched on a sundial was a raven. Jo recalled the solitary bird which had seemed to watch them on their visit to Dozmary Pool, and she realised the countryside must have been full of spies under the spell of this wicked lady.

Sensing her thoughts, Morgana began to speak. "When a shattering explosion erupts in the sea a few miles behind *La Mirabelle* at the precise moment when two bombs are detonated, it does not take a sorceress to work out that the trunks must have contained something—or someone—else."

The girls were once again in despair, and as the blue van set off towards Glastonbury, they could not help but wonder what had happened to Hilda.

Jake regained consciousness to find he was looking at the grinning face of Cabhan, with James looking concerned behind him.

"A top quality sword, don't you think?" asked the craftsman proudly, and Jake nodded in agreement. The slain dog was still beside him, and all around lay the remains of the ferocious pack. The sight of such carnage, in particular the motionless creature beside him, caused Jake to turn away and vomit.

"You are not the first warrior to be sick after battle, Jake," said Sir Lancelot, "and I am sure you will not be the last. You have done well." These words from the great warrior made him feel a lot better.

Sir Tristram had decided his company should have a short rest before going any farther, and James took the opportunity to ask Merlin about the Hunter, who had vanished from the scene. He had sent his hounds into battle but had withdrawn himself back into the shadows.

"The Hunter serves the goddess in her Underworld, the gateway to which is in the Island of the Dead. He sweeps the marshes for souls of the departed in order to select those that will be brought to her for rebirth. The

Nine Keepers, of whom Rhiannon is one, guard the mysteries of Avalon and oversee the energies of the Zodiac."

"Zodiac? Do you mean the signs like Leo and Capricorn, the reading of horoscopes and all that?"

"Precisely. Gathered tightly around the tor itself, the earth has each sign of the Zodiac carved into its surface. In this way, the goddess and her Keepers hold some mystical power over life's destiny—a power that very few are able to challenge."

"Are you one of those few, Merlin?" asked Jake.

"Indeed I am, Jake, but I need the assistance of other magic, such as Excalibur, if I am to have influence over the goddess herself."

"And the Lady of the Lake? Does she also possess this power?" asked James.

"Yes. Her magic is stronger than mine, and her knowledge is deeper. There is one other who could challenge the Zodiac and the Keepers, one other who has been studying and perfecting the arts of witchcraft."

"Don't tell me—let me guess," said James. "Morgana Le Fay?"

Merlin nodded, his face expressionless.

A thought formed in James's mind, and he was beginning to make some sense of all that had been happening during recent days. He excitedly put his theory to Merlin. "Is it possible Morgana Le Fay might have some power beyond this Earth?"

"You speak in riddles," James.

"Exactly! The reason our father had to go back to London was a riddle threatening our country. It may be that this riddle was sent by Morgan!"

"Do you remember the words of this riddle?"

"Yes, and I've been trying to work it out ever since." He remembered it word for word.

> "Island people, give way to the force
> That decrees your awful fate:
> A shooting star is set on course
> To explode in the midst of your state."

James asked hesitantly, "Merlin, might the island be Avalon?"

"It is possible. Was there more?"

OLRIC!

> "When Rangoma's Comet lights the sky,
> All of Britain rests.
> The future king will surely die
> Midst explosions in the west."

"Rangoma? There is no comet under that name. But wait—*Rangoma* is an anagram of *Morgana*. You are asking me, James, if she has the power to create a shooting star? Yes, she probably has that power now. Even if she is not able to control it as well, she could call upon someone with an understanding of physics to help her."

"What about the future king?" asked Jake.

Merlin was silent, apparently lost in thought.

"I have heard a reference to King Arthur as 'the Once and Future King'," said James.

"By the mysteries of the Zodiac, I do believe you have it!" exclaimed Merlin. "It all points to Morgana Le Fay. Was there more?"

> "Missiles and bombs will cross the shore
> And western power diminish.
> Britain's Kingdom will be no more,
> Its relevance extinguished."

"Yes," said the wizard. "People do not refer to Britain's kingdom now, for it is known as the United Kingdom. Arthur was king of the *Britons*. Morgana Le Fay is certainly involved with modern terrorists, but she still wages a personal war with the Great King. There is no time to waste before Avalon is destroyed. We must march on!"

Chapter 14

The Thorn Delivers

They had reached the end of the marshes, and the tor began to loom out of the mist in front of them. In the foreground rose the ruins of the abbey, parts of a great stone skeleton hinting of its magnificence in times past. Even in ruins, there was a majestic splendour about the place, the sheer height of the arch dwarfing all around it. In the moonlight, there was a ghostly pale sheen which lit the stone walls and pillars—until everything went dark all of a sudden, as if the light was switched off.

At first, James and Jake thought a cloud had covered the moon, yet it still shone weakly in the clear sky. The reason for the darkness was the dense flock of birds—mostly crows, jackdaws, and magpies—settling on the ruins while others flew in huge, swirling clouds around them. The beating of their wings made a deafening sound around the stillness of the abbey. *Wow!* thought James. *I think they must be preparing to attack!* He shuddered, recalling the horrifying battle on the cliffs when they had returned from Dozmary Pool. At the highest point of the abbey stood a solitary raven, the bird of ill omen poised, as if ready to give the command to swoop down on the invaders.

Suddenly, a loud, echoing roar came out of the shadows beyond, and slowly a hostile band of moorogs emerged in battle formation, axes swinging menacingly as they approached.

"Yield, pagan scum, before your blood stains this holy ground!" The challenge was issued by Sir Lancelot, and his bold words gave heart to all the knights, who cheered loudly. The moorogs stopped in their tracks, apparently surprised by the response to their threatened attack.

OLRIC!

"Come, let us clear this filth from our path!" shouted Sir Lancelot, and with Sir Gawain at his side, he led the knights forward into battle. Jake and James, who remained behind with Cabhan, were thrilled by the excitement of seeing these ancient warriors riding fearlessly forward to fight their enemies.

The moorogs turned and fled in a shambolic rabble whilst every crow flapped its wings and abandoned the ruins amidst a hideous raucous chorus, flying up into the sky to settle loudly in an untidy mass at the summit of the tor. The knights returned to find a troubled Merlin sitting in council with Sir Tristram.

The joy of victory was short-lived with the knights realising the animosity and power this situation had brought, which was well beyond their understanding and experience.

"Why did they stand aside?" wondered the Sir Tristram aloud.

Merlin replied, "Maybe it is a trap. They know our business and will think we shall drop our guard in this moment of victory. They still have the power and sorcery to destroy our mission, so we must be cautious as well as courageous."

A brief silence fell over the knights as they thought about Merlin's wise words.

"We can't just wait, Merlin," said Sir Tristram after a few moments, the hunger for combat still showing in his eyes. "I think we should fight now!" His words inspired a loud cheer of support from many of his companions.

"All our enemies are up there," said Sir Bors. "We could surround them and then storm the tor." The thought of going into battle again made both James and Jake feel scared, and they huddled closer together behind the reassuring presence of Merlin.

"They would have the advantage of being on higher ground. Besides, we cannot be sure all our foes are there. It might be a trap, and there may be others waiting to attack us unexpectedly," countered Sir Lancelot.

"We must not forget that there are mystic powers deep within the tor," added Sir Percival. "Courage and strength alone may not be enough to win the day." While the debate continued, a widespread muttering could be heard amongst the knights, most of whom favoured an attack on the Tor.

"To sit in council shows weakness," said Sir Gawain impatiently. "We have come to fight, and if I must fight alone, then so be it! I am going to attack the vermin awaiting us!" After saying this, he began to stride purposefully away, and James could sense his lust for battle.

Merlin rose and stood tall and commandingly over the assembled knights, booming a loud rebuke in the direction of Sir Gawain. "Come back! Listen to what I have to say." The departing warrior stopped and reluctantly returned to join his companions. The wizard continued, his voice raised with authority. "Evil sorcery is at work before us and in our midst. Can you not see that the unity of the Round Table is being challenged? If we argue, we are only playing into her hands."

"What steps do you suggest now, Merlin?" asked Sir Percival.

"We do what we came to do. There is only one way in which we can re-establish the unity of the Round Table: we must summon the Great King and also those lying at rest with him."

"You speak wisely, Merlin. We are far beyond the boundaries of my land. At Tintagel of old and now in Lyonesse, I am ruler, and it is my word that is to be obeyed. But we need the authority of a greater man, who has the strength to pull his men together in unity from the widest outposts of this land."

Merlin looked him in the eye and grasped the knight's hand in his, acknowledging his honest humility. Then he bowed before turning away once more to address all those who stood around him. "Come, valiant knights, and stand in the centre of the abbey's ruins, forming one great circle." While the knights followed the wizard's command, he turned his attention towards the boys. "James and Jake, you must stand beside me inside the circle while these brave warriors take their places around us."

While slowly lifting Excalibur, still in its scabbard, Merlin led the way within the walls of the abbey and stood facing east, where the High Altar would once have been. He beckoned James to stand on his right and Jake on his left, while twenty-two knights formed a wide circle facing inwards around them.

"Present your swords!" commanded the wizard, and twenty-two blades flashed in the moonlight. "Yours too," he added, and the two brothers raised their swords. An overwhelming sense of pride enveloped them as they were aware of the magical importance of this moment and the part they were now playing in a living legend. Merlin closed his eyes, raising his head to the stars before he opened them once more. He grasped the hilt of Excalibur and slowly drew the magnificent, gleaming blade into the

OLRIC!

open. A gasp could be heard from the assembled company as he held the sword up in front of him. A bolt of lightning flashed from the blade, and there was a powerful gust of wind which threatened to blow the company off their feet. As the wind passed, Merlin stood firm and bellowed out a cry which could have been heard far beyond the marshes.

> "Yomar! Yomar! Awaken, beasts of the Zodiac:
> Leo! Virgo! Libra! Scorpio! Waken from your leisure.
> Sagittarius! Capricorn! Aquarius! Pisces, too, in equal measure!
> Aries! Taurus! Gemini! Cancer! Yield up your treasure!
> With this sword, Excalibur, I call upon the son of Pendragon,
> That he may join us in spirit and that he may rise again, as decreed of old!
> Arthur, King of all Britain, return and lead us in this final quest!"

A hush descended over the abbey while the men continued to stand motionless in the circle, their swords firmly held before them, awaiting something to happen. All of a sudden, there was light, and the two boys looked round to see where it had come from.

To their amazement, it was the Glastonbury Thorn Tree, which was lit like a Christmas decoration in Piccadilly. Each of its twisted branches glowed in a white light, and every thorn gleamed with a soft golden glow. The vision was so bright that James and Jake had to shield their eyes. All the knights around them sunk silently to their knees, their heads bowed. The boys also knelt, not quite knowing why, but they were unable to resist looking at the tree.

Amongst the branches, human shapes began to form, and slowly they emerged from what had become a burning bush, its flames leaping high into the night sky. The group of shapes moved majestically towards them. Their unhurried steps gave the two boys time to absorb every detail: the leader was a man clad in a red cloak, its hems of emerald green. His blond hair and beard were of medium length, and on his head he wore a simple golden crown. This was the figure of legend whose stories had captivated listeners for hundreds of years, whose courage and ideals had been admired like those of a god. King Arthur himself had stepped out of the flames to lead his people once more.

The Thorn Delivers

At his side was Queen Guinevere, her jet-black hair hanging loosely over her shoulders. She wore a faded golden dress inlaid with jewels, and her face radiated a beauty that would soften the hardest of hearts. Bringing up the rear were three knights dressed for battle. As the boys were soon to find out, these were among the holiest of all to sit at the Round Table: Sir Gareth, Sir Bedivere, and Sir Galahad.

The silence was broken by one simple word, uttered in a loud, commanding voice by King Arthur for the first time in over a thousand years. "Arise!" The majestic command echoed around the ruins of the old abbey.

All around the boys, there were tears of joy as the men rose to their feet, clashing their swords with one another in salute of their leader.

"Will you not step back, good knights, and make space for us to widen the circle?" Arthur's words were more humbly spoken this time, but they carried an authority which would not be questioned. The king moved forward once more, followed by the three men who had also emerged from the thorn tree. Guinevere was ushered through to join Merlin in the centre of the circle, and the boys gazed up at her sparkling eyes, which lingered over them for a moment before she looked round at the assembled might of the Round Table.

The Glastonbury Thorn was no longer ablaze. Now that it had delivered its precious souls, the tree merely stood unnoticed in the darkness, its gnarled and twisted branches drooping in the gentle breeze, while the men assembled in the abbey's ruins greeted each other in joyous celebration.

"If only Jo were here with us," said Jake to his brother. "She would have loved this."

"You're so right," replied James. "Once we've won this battle, these knights will ride to rescue her from Morgana Le Fay."

"Do not forget you also have swords," said Cabhan. "You may be able to rescue her yourselves." James and Jake looked at each other with trepidation, but Cabhan continued. "And you can count on my support as well." He smiled and put a hand on each of their shoulders before he withdrew into the shadows.

"You are not of our time, are you?" The boys were startled to hear a voice which was new to them, a voice which almost sang in a light melodic tone from the Welsh valleys. They turned to face Queen Guinevere, who

OLRIC!

was reaching out towards them, her soft, warm eyes looking at them beneath long lashes.

"No, we are not, Your Majesty," replied James. "But we are here to serve the king."

"We went to fetch Excalibur," said Jake, as usual eager to get in on the act, but he only achieved a cold stare from his brother.

"If that is the case, you have already fulfilled your quest, and you were well chosen for the task. Few would have been able to prise the great sword from the hidden depths of Dozmary Pool and deliver it safely to Merlin." Guinevere smiled and fixed the boys with a tenderness that seemed to penetrate the deepest parts of their minds whilst filling their hearts with pride.

"You're very kind," said James, "but we can't claim to have fulfilled anything until we've rescued Jo."

"Jo?"

"Our sister," explained Jake. "She's been taken prisoner by Morgana Le Fay."

At this, Guinevere's expression changed to one of anxiety and she looked at the boys with concern written across her worried face. "Tell me how this came about." She sat down, beckoning James and Jake to join her. While King Arthur and his knights sat in council, Guinevere listened to the boys' tale of how they had become involved in the quest to reunite the Round Table. They described how Jo had been captured at the battle, how Madame Lafayette had revealed her true identity, and how Excalibur had been protected from her evil forces. As their story unfolded, nothing troubled Guinevere as much as the description of Olric. James thought she must have had a deep fear of birds of prey because she seemed to tremble at the description of how the buzzard had attacked Jo outside the cave.

By the time the boys had finished telling their tale, the circle of knights had broken up. The strategy for battle had been decided, and everywhere men were preparing to advance on the tor, their faces glowing with enthusiasm at the prospect of reclaiming the Isle of Avalon from the darkness of the dead. With King Arthur wielding Excalibur once again, nothing could stand in their way.

Merlin was puzzled. It was unusual for the wizard to be confused or at a loss, and now he was both of those. He had succeeded in seeing that

Excalibur was returned safely into his care, as well as guiding the men from Lyonesse to awaken King Arthur, but part of the Lady's riddle was still unclear.

> Seek the eagle as before,
> When moonlight sweeps across the tor:
> There will be pointed,
> As Joseph anointed,
> The Chalice, as told in folklore.

The moonlight was faint, but it was still capable of casting light over the tor. There was no sign of an eagle, however, so Merlin wondered if the boys had correctly remembered the words spoken to them at Dozmary Pool. He called them over to him and asked that very question.

"Are you absolutely sure you remembered the words of the Lady of the Lake? I see no signs of eagles here, and you should know eagles are not seen in these southern parts."

"I know we're right, Merlin," said Jake. "We *are* right, aren't we, James?"

"A hundred per cent," agreed his brother. "But hang on—there's something you said, Merlin ..."

"Something *I* said? Whatever do you mean?"

"You said *no sign* of an eagle. Perhaps we should look for a sign or emblem, rather than the bird itself."

"Of course! What blindness made me miss such an interpretation? James, you may have the answer to this riddle!" While Merlin summoned as many knights as he could see to search for any sign of eagles, James beamed with pride at having possibly solved a riddle which had proved to be beyond the wit of a wizard.

A short while later, there was a triumphant shout from the direction of a ruined arch, close to the altar of the old abbey. It was Sir Percival, and as Merlin approached in answer to the call, he could see the knight's face was illuminated by a shaft of moonlight. Sir Percival stared intensely at an eagle carved into the stone pillar.

"The eagle as before, when moonlight sweeps across the tor!"

Merlin looked closely at the carving and read out loud the words in Latin inscribed beneath it.

"*Aquila Legionis Decimae*— Eagle of the Tenth Legion! This is a carving of the standard of the Roman Legion, which came to these shores with Julius Caesar in 55BC, and these words tell the story of the invasion!"

King Arthur had followed the group through the ruins. "Merlin, can you explain what this eagle is hiding? What part has it to play in our quest?"

"The eagle BC—before Christ! Your Majesty, this is 'the eagle as before'!"

"How did the riddle continue?"

"'There will be pointed, as Joseph anointed, the Chalice, as told in folklore,'" piped up Jake, causing everyone to look round at him. Everyone, that was, except Sir Galahad, whose eyes stared closely at the carved inscriptions.

"Pointed," he said in a deep, assertive voice. "Somewhere hidden in this stone lies the Chalice, the Holy Grail, which was brought to this sacred place by Joseph of Arimethea."

"Wow! Unreal! The Holy Grail!" said both boys together.

"Hidden? Or carved?" questioned Merlin, whose attention had been brought back to the pillar. "Might it not be an *image* of the Grail, rather than the Chalice itself?"

"In which case, could *this* be what we seek?" asked Sir Bedivere, who pointed to a carved picture of a small and simple goblet. It had no handle, but the perfectly curved shape held a mysterious quality about it, and Merlin thought there was something almost familiar about it. He could not think why that should be, unless it was the picture of the Holy Grail which he had always imagined in his innermost thoughts. Then the memory struck him of where he had seen the goblet before, and he lightly touched the carving, quietly murmuring words in an unknown tongue.

There was not a soul amongst the assembled company who doubted this was indeed the image for which they had been seeking, and all the men around the pillar knelt in silent prayer at the foot of the pillar. Merlin, however, continued to wonder where the real Holy Grail was hidden because this was only a carving of it.

Sir Lancelot looked up when he heard a noise like the marching of ten thousand feet coming from the far side of the tor. All around, knights stopped in their tracks as the noise grew louder, and they gathered to stare up at the tower on the tor's summit, waiting for a sign from their enemies.

They did not need to wait long. The cause of the marching "feet" had come not from an army of foot soldiers but from the beating wings of countless birds. Now the enormous flock was rising from the far side of the hill, led by a solitary black raven, casting a vast black cloud over the vale. As the leading birds soared up far into the night sky, still the dark feathered squadrons continued to rise behind the tor.

James and Jake, still in the company of Guinevere, gazed up with fear and dread at this show of strength from Morgana's evil forces. The knights remained spellbound by the sheer mass of birds which had taken to the air.

Then the birds swooped down low, an immense tidal wave of feathers driven by the beating of wings, which deafened King Arthur's men as they flung themselves to the ground to escape the sweeping frenzy of the attack.

Chapter 15

Damsels in Distress

The blue van pulled off the main road and stopped a little way along a rough track. Jo and Lola were roughly dragged out and made to stand facing Morgana Le Fay, their hands held tightly behind their backs by McCulloch. A look of evil loathing burned from the woman's eyes as she addressed the two prisoners.

"Look over there," she commanded, indicating to her right, "and you will see a hill." The girls' eyes followed the direction of her outstretched arm and they could make out the shape of the hill, with a tower at the top. "On the other side of that hill, your brothers are waiting."

"My brothers?" asked Jo incredulously. "Waiting for what?"

"For death."

"Death?" Jo could not come to terms with this news. It was yet another dreadful twist of the knife held by the woman who had appeared to be so kind when they had met only days before. "How can they be waiting for death?" she cried. "You can't let them die! What have they done to deserve that?"

"What else can they expect when they have interfered with my plans and have chosen to be amongst knights who are not welcome in Avalon, the Isle of the Dead? So stop snivelling, you pathetic little brat."

"Sir Lancelot and his men will not allow my brothers to die." Jo spoke with hope, but inwardly she feared the worst. *What if they have already been captured, and the knights are prisoners and unable to come to their aid?* She looked at Lola for reassurance, but the other girl's head was bowed.

Jo turned back to face her captor, who seemed to be delighting in mental torture.

"So be it. We shall see!" Morgana Le Fay cackled nastily as she paused. "We're going to the top of the hill, following a path unknown to mortal men, up seven levels through a maze of ancient mystery. If anyone tries to follow us, they will die."

When she had said this, the girls were led across the field and began the slow ascent towards the top of the tor. The path they trod was as secret as Morgana had said, weaving up through the dark of the night. She led the way, and McCulloch followed the two girls, making sure they did not run away. Escape would have been impossible in any case. On each side of the path, they could see eyes and hear sounds of unimaginably horrible creatures, prowling in the hope of catching any unsuspecting prey which veered away from safety.

As they wound their way nearer to the top, there was a deafening din of flapping wings all around them. A seemingly solid block of birds, mostly crows, took off and flew noisily overhead before swooping out of sight over the tor. Jo shivered, scared by the endless number of wings. She glanced at Lola, who looked back at her, her face reflecting her own fear.

"We are nearly there," announced Morgan triumphantly, and in front of them the girls could make out the eerie shape of a strange tower. Close by, a camp fire burned. Around it was gathered a large number of primitive-looking men ready for battle, and a little farther along the ridge, Jo recognised the terrifying sight of countless axes, gleaming in the moonlight. Moorogs! There was no chance of escape. McCulloch grabbed both girls roughly by the neck and marched them towards a single post which had been stuck firmly into the ground. At the foot of the post was a boulder. With the aid of another cruel-looking man, McCulloch stood them on the boulder and bound them back-to-back round the post.

As the rope cut into their flesh, Jo and Lola attempted to turn away from their captors. They were trying to work out why they were being treated like this when, to their horror, they saw others approaching with sticks and branches. These were placed around them by evil, merciless men who were sneering and leering hideously into their terrified eyes. They were going to be burned like witches at the stake!

When the birds had passed, King Arthur and his knights rose slowly to their feet and watched the swarming flock fly into the west until it became no more than a black cloud on the horizon.

"Will they come back?" asked Jake to no one in particular.

"Without a doubt," replied Cabhan, who had appeared at his shoulder. "Next time it may be to attack."

"They will not be alone," added Sir Tristram, looking back towards the tor. Then he exclaimed in surprise, "Look! Look up there!" When all his companions looked up behind them, they could see a line of figures silhouetted against the early dawn sky. The figures were standing and looking down onto the flat plain below them, and a fire was burning close to the tower. A little farther away, there was an unlit bonfire round a stake, and those with the keenest eyesight could distinguish two prisoners bound to it.

An execution was about to take place, and all the king's army could do was stand and watch.

A raven flew down from the tor, its wings flapping slowly in an ominous way. As it approached the abbey ruins, it glided down towards Merlin and dropped a piece of paper in front of him before climbing once more and heading back towards the tower. Merlin knelt to pick up the paper. A worried expression came over his face as he read the note written on it, and he gazed up at the figures on the skyline.

"This is a threat from Morgana Le Fay. She has two children held as hostages," he announced briefly. "One of them is Jo." At this, James and Jake gasped, but the wizard continued. "If we do not leave this place before sunrise, they will light the brushwood round the stake."

These words were greeted with horror, but there seemed to be no alternative other than to give in. The men turned to King Arthur for his command.

"How long do we have?" asked Sir Lancelot.

"It is of no matter," replied King Arthur. "We do not leave until the victory is ours. We attack!"

"Your Majesty, those are children up there. We cannot let them die!" pleaded Sir Lancelot, and there was a murmur of agreement from many of the other knights.

"Brave knights, fellows of the Round Table," answered the king with authority, his voice reaching every one of his men, "do you really believe that a sorceress as evil as Morgana Le Fay would honour her word? Those children will die whether or not we obey her command. Is there a man amongst you who honestly believes she will release her prisoners if we turn and leave this place? The torch will be lit and the fire kindled as soon as we are out of sight!"

Nobody could bring himself to disagree with the wise words of the king. Silence followed as they stood awaiting his next command.

"Your Majesty." Again it was Sir Lancelot who spoke. "At least give us the chance to save them, I beg you. There are men around us who earned their spurs in the fairest age of time through rescuing damsels in distress. Let us try to free these children!"

"Indeed you shall free them, Lancelot," said King Arthur. "That is my command. Take whoever you need and lie out of sight, preparing to storm the tor. The rest of us will start to retreat. As soon as you reach the summit, we shall return and ride to your assistance."

Sir Lancelot bowed in gratitude and walked back to gather his chosen companions. He enlisted Sir Gawain, Sir Galahad, and Sir Bors. While the four knights withdrew to discuss their plan of attack, the rest of the king's army began to retreat once more through the marshes to the west.

Merlin thought it better not to remind the men they were turning back towards the crows, who had flown over them in such huge numbers. The birds would be sure to pick them off like carrion if they were to fly back eastwards. While Merlin was lost in these thoughts, his worries increased when Guinevere appeared at his side.

"James and Jake," she said urgently. "They are not amongst us. They have disappeared!"

―⁂―

While Arthur led his troops away from the abbey, the two boys lay on the dark side of the tor. As soon as they had heard their sister was not

OLRIC!

only nearby but in mortal danger, they had stolen away into the shadows without being noticed.

All they had to do was climb the hill, and they would free Jo from the dreadful fate awaiting her. It no longer seemed so straightforward as they lay watching King Arthur's knights retreating, apparently yielding to the demands of the enemy.

"Even if we do free Jo, where can we take her to safety?" whispered Jake. "The knights have all left."

"We'll find a way," said his brother. "We can't give up now."

"Let's go, then! Anyway, I want to see who the other prisoner is!"

"Which route shall we take?" asked Sir Galahad.

"The western slope will be in shadow," said Sir Bors. "We are less likely to be seen."

"That's too steep for the horses. How about coming from the south?" suggested Sir Gawain. "We shall need horses for a swift escape."

"It is agreed, then," stated Sir Lancelot. "We do not have time for further discussion if we are to rescue those girls. We lead the horses under cover of darkness to the south side. Then we shall climb. Come."

Once at the foot of the hill, they quietly mounted the horses and walked cautiously forward, hoping the enemy would be looking at the army in retreat across the marshes. As they climbed, the crimson glow of dawn spread from the east, and the knights were aware they were bound to be seen. They urged their horses into a trot and then a canter, and they began their charge at full gallop towards the bonfire.

The boys had almost reached the top and lay looking ahead to see how they might free the prisoners. Their spirits sank, however, when they saw how many men and moorogs there were. Close by, the fire still burned. Morgana Le Fay, her face seeming witchlike above the flames, was looking over their heads in the direction of the marshes.

"Good. They have gone," she said. "Even with Excalibur, they do not have the spirit for a fight. McCulloch, take the flame to the stake, and we shall reward our followers with the sound of those girls screaming. As the smoke envelopes them, the fire will reduce their feeble bodies to ashes!"

The host of moorogs spread out to form a wide circle round the bonfire, and the primitive sound of their jeer-snorting sent more shivers down the spines of the two helpless girls. They watched McCulloch approaching them through the ring of moorogs and brandishing a torch of flaming brushwood.

James looked at Jake. Their hopes were dashed by the sight of so many moorogs, and time had run out for them to crawl unnoticed to the stake. In a few seconds, the flames would be roaring up around their sister, and there would be nothing they could do to help her.

"Listen!" said James excitedly. He did not need to say more because the sound of galloping hooves was unmistakable above the ghastly din of bloodthirsty moorogs. The boys watched, amazed, as four mounted knights charged into the breaking circle and were soon surrounded by their enemies. Axe clashed with blade, but the knights at least had the benefit of surprise to their advantage.

"Light the fire!" shrieked Morgana Le Fay, and McCulloch pushed the torch into the pile of dry branches.

As smoke began to drift up and small flames danced close to the feet of the girls, James and Jake sprinted from their cover. In the confusion, no one saw them running towards the fire. So determined were the moorogs to prevent the knights from getting to the victims that the way was clear for the boys.

Lola and Jo were screaming now, the heat beginning to reach their ankles and the smoke penetrating their nostrils. In their agony, they were beginning to lose consciousness.

Jo thought she was hallucinating when she saw her brothers enter the clearing, their new swords at the ready. Seconds later, the boys had cut through the bonds tying the girls to the stake, and they dragged them away from the fire before it began to roar in a ferocious blaze. All four of them lay coughing in a heap and had neither the time nor the strength to run further to safety.

The sense of victory was short-lived. James managed to look up in search of a route to safety, and he saw McCulloch approaching with a long spear in one hand and an axe in the other. The man's face was twisted in hatred, and he bellowed in fury while he charged towards the four children.

McCulloch's gruesome expression never changed, but the bellowing ceased as his head rolled from his shoulders. His bleeding body fell crashing to the ground. Behind him was Sir Lancelot, his sword dripping with blood, and he steered his horse over to the children, closely followed by the other three knights.

Without wasting any time on words, the knights hauled the four children into the saddles. They galloped away through the broken ranks of moorogs and down the slope, back to the sanctuary of the abbey. King Arthur and his army returned from their mock flight to see the fire raging on the tor. McCulloch's corpse was burning with a number of moorogs which had been slain by the knights. The stench of flaming flesh drifted down in the half-light of the dawn.

Later, Cabhan was smiling at James as he regained consciousness, his lungs heaving with indignation at the amount of smoke he'd inhaled while cutting through the bonds at the stake.

"Is Jo all right?" James enquired.

"Yes, they are all going to recover, James, although Jo and the other girl breathed in a lot more smoke than you. Merlin is treating them with potions which will clear their lungs. The fumes would have killed them, even before the flames had consumed their bodies."

James lay back, happy in the knowledge they were all safe, at least for now. Sir Lancelot entered the tent followed by the three knights who had accompanied him up to the tor, as well as by King Arthur. They beamed broadly at him and his younger brother, who was also coughing himself back to life.

"Thank you," said James. "That's the third time you've saved our lives."

"We have not come to receive your thanks," replied the French knight. "We are here in the presence of royalty to proclaim your courage, and to praise you for saving the damsels."

"We would never have reached them in time," added Sir Galahad.

"James and Jake," announced King Arthur, "I salute you. You were well chosen to assist in this quest, and your bravery has made sure of our victory in this first battle. You have earned the right to stand alongside us. The conflict will be fiercer than ever before the end of this day."

"Game on!" murmured Jake, smiling weakly before his eyes closed once more. "This is unreal!"

Chapter 16

The Battle of Avalon Vale

Morgana Le Fay was furious. She had planned the public execution of the captured girls as a morale boost for her followers and a timely reminder of her own ruthlessness. Her enemies would never have recovered from their failure to save two children, and any who doubted would have realised she held the upper hand in seeking control over Earth's destiny.

Now she had seen her prisoners released not only by the accursed knights of King Arthur's Round Table but also by the raw spirit of two other children who were continuing to interfere in her plans. Her rage calmed, however, when she realised this had only been a minor setback (if an embarrassing one) in her bid for supremacy. By her reckoning, all four children would be dead by nightfall.

Her army of men and moorogs already outnumbered the knights, and soon the massive number of birds would return, heralding the arrival of her own special fighting force. In addition, she also had allies in those who guarded the Isle of the Dead: Annwn herself, her Keepers, and the Hunter, who still had the pride of his pack to unleash.

While she watched King Arthur leading his men back into the ruined abbey, she smiled in the knowledge that she held the higher ground. Victory would come swiftly and without mercy, and she could turn her attention to establishing control over the world's nations.

Once Rangoma's Comet exploded here in the spiritual centre of Britain, no one would have cause to doubt the meaning of "missiles and bombs will cross the shore'" no one would know who lay behind such devastation, but people would soon look beyond Europe and start to blame the rising powers in the east. Retribution would be demanded and war would follow, causing enormous loss of life around the globe as she, Morgana Le Fay, rose from the ashes of destruction. Unchallenged, she would mould the destiny of the planet to suit her needs, and she would revel in the ruthless annihilation of Earth's civilisations.

The boys were talking proudly to Cabhan, describing their dawn raid and rescue of the girls. The blacksmith listened with excitement and enjoyed the moment when McCulloch's head had parted from his shoulders. He was also pleased his craftsmanship had created the boys' swords, which had cut so quickly through the rope binding the girls.

"Did I not say you might go to Jo's rescue?"

"Yes, you did," said James, "but I didn't believe you at the time. Not in the company of kings and knights, who are so much stronger and braver than us."

"No one questions your bravery, James," said Merlin, who had come to join them. The two girls were with him, and Jo embraced her brothers as if she hadn't seen them for years.

"I can't believe it!" she said. "I wondered if I was ever going to see you again!"

"We were hoping the same thing," joked Jake, earning a punch in the ribs from his sister, who turned to introduce her companion.

"You'll never guess who this is," she said. The boys looked suitably blank, and Jo was about to continue when the other girl spoke.

"Hi! I'm Lola Mendes."

Once this surprise had sunk in, Jo told her brothers how she had woken to find herself on *La Mirabelle* in the company of the missing girl. She also explained how her fleece had been taken out of her room. James and Jake listened to the two girls interrupting one another in their excitement to tell the story of their failed attempt to escape from the boat, the cruelty of Morgana Le Fay, and the unexpected help from Hilda leading to their journeys by train.

"We really thought we were dead when she held the knife in front of us," said Lola, who then went on to describe her journey in the trunk. "At first I was scared, but then it seemed so cool until I began to wonder if I'd

OLRIC!

ever get out. I seemed to have spent so much time tied up in a dark space that I thought I'd never see daylight again!"

"It was hard to trust Hilda. Ever since we'd first met her, she'd always seemed to hate us. And we all thought she was Morgana Le Fay, didn't we?" Jo wasn't expecting an answer to this question, and she went on. "Allowing ourselves to be locked into a trunk and then be loaded onto a dinghy was really worrying. If I hadn't heard the men talking, I'd have thought I was floating alone on the sea."

"Me too," added Lola. "They didn't half swear carrying us ashore. I've learned at least three new words!"

"They must have taken us up through the secret tunnel from the cave to Penmarrett," said Jo. "Hilda was talking to the men, and I still couldn't understand whether she was helping us to escape or sending us to our deaths when they loaded us into the van."

"What was it like on the train?" asked Jake.

"Not too bad, really," said Lola. "It was nice to hear the sound of people talking."

"I didn't like it," said Jo. "I so wanted to get out and tell everyone what I was doing there, but I knew we both had to sit tight until we were well away from those horrible men."

"I think you're both incredibly brave," acknowledged James generously. "Apart from everything else, you must have suffered from claustrophobia in such a confined space."

"I expect so," agreed Lola uncertainly. She wasn't yet used to James's advanced use of vocabulary.

"We must have got split up at Exeter," said Jo, returning to the story, "because I could hear Lola's trunk being dragged out. We always knew where we were because of the announcements at each station. When my train drew into Birmingham, I could sense it was a really big place because of the noise. Then I heard the order being given to evacuate, followed by the fire alarm. At first I didn't realise it was all because of my trunk!"

"Same with me," said Lola. "I couldn't wait to get out. It was the same at Reading: 'All personnel to the nearest exits—the station is to be evacuated.' And there was my trunk, sitting all on its own on the train!"

"I suppose they had to evacuate just in case there was a bomb," said Jo, "but they were expecting to find you at Reading after Sergeant

Cruickshank discovered me. He said I was the most welcome stick of dynamite he'd ever seen!"

"Obviously doesn't know you very well then!" said Jake, earning another punch from his sister.

The king and Sir Tristram looked up at the tor, wondered when the enemy was going to attack, and planned their strategy for defence. They agreed they were too heavily outnumbered to face a siege in the abbey, and to launch an attack up the hill would simply play into Morgan's hands.

"We could surround the tor and make them feel *they* were being besieged," suggested Sir Tristram.

"Our forces would be too thinly spread, and they would know it. We could pretend to retreat and lure them down to the vale. At least that way we would fight on the same level."

They had no chance to make any preparations because a shout above them was followed by a spine-chilling roar and the waving of a thousand axes. The enemy was coming down the slope towards them. The battle had begun!

Moorogs were advancing in their customary crescent, seeking to outflank the knights, who rapidly mounted their horses to give them the advantage of height and speed over their enemy. As a dark cloud drifted across the sun, the dawn turned to grey. Strange shadows swept down the hillside.

The Moorogs shrieked out their challenge in a frenzied chant, which reminded Jo and Lola of their plight up on the summit, when the torch had been put to the bonfire. For the time being, at least, they were surrounded by friends and made sure they stayed close to James and Jake, who proudly held their swords in readiness for the attack.

While Sir Lancelot led the defence against the centre of the moorog crescent, Sir Gawain led a section on the left and Sir Percival's men defended the right flank. The sheer ferocity of these knights took the moorogs by surprise. Not a knight was lost as hordes of the evil creatures fell in a mass of snorting, screeching chaos. The attack had been successfully repelled, but a shout came from the rearguard:

OLRIC!

"Dogs to the west!" Looking back over the marshes, King Arthur could see a pack of large white hounds swarming through the reeds over the swamp. They were baying in search of their quarry, and in their midst ran the Hunter, his long spear held out before him as he yelled words of encouragement to his fierce pack.

"Merlin!" called the king of the Britons, "do we have any defence over these wolves of the underworld?"

"They fear fire, Your Majesty," answered the wizard, and he waved his staff in the direction of the advancing hounds. "Shadaihkay!" he shouted above the din of battle. A line of orange and red flames sprung up out the turf, causing the hounds to stop, baring their fangs in frustration at being thwarted.

Guinevere pointed to the top of the tor, where the figure of Morgana Le Fay stood triumphantly watching the battle below. She had been joined by nine other figures, each one a lady in shape and each one ghostlike in form, their bodies darkly opaque in the morning sunlight.

"The Keepers!" uttered Merlin in despair. "So the Guardians of the Dead *have* sided with Morgan after all! This was beyond my darkest fear!"

"Merlin, who are the Keepers?" asked Jo.

"They are the Keepers of the Mysteries, Jo. Like the Hunter, they serve the goddess of the Underworld and have power over the living and the dead. Your brothers have already met one of them on the way here; James was almost led into the lands of the dead by Rhiannon, but he was saved just in time. Now Rhiannon is amongst her fellow guardians, Vivien, Anu and Danu, Arianrhod and Cerridwen, Morrigu, Epona, and Rigantona. Their presence on the battlefield is ill news, and I fear the nine will soon start casting their spells down amongst our men in the vale."

"Can you do anything to stop them?" asked Lola.

"I have no power over the Keepers or over any who serve the goddess. If Morgan has her as an ally, no magic of mine can defeat her." The children watched with disbelief as the wizard of legend appeared to stoop like a helpless, crippled old man before their very eyes. Guinevere went to him and seemed to whisper some words of encouragement, which caused him to look up once more with a glimmer of a spark in his eyes, but he remained as the image of a broken man, a wizard who had finally reached the end of the road.

The Battle of Avalon Vale

The Hunter and his pack of hounds were kept at bay by the hot wall of flames, and the abbey was echoing with the howls and screams of battle as swords flashed and axes crashed loudly against shields. The children watched as the nine Keepers began to descend from the tor. Like phantoms in a nightmare, they walked down through the ranks of moorogs, their eyes locked in a trance on the beleaguered group of knights and children within the abbey walls.

"Look over there!" shouted James, remembering his earlier experience with Rhiannon. "We've got to escape from those spooks before they put a spell on us."

It was then the children saw exactly why the name of King Arthur had survived at the head of all the nation's heroes through the mists of time. First, he caught a riderless horse fleeing from the field of battle and mounted it in one swift movement. He charged headlong into the mass of moorogs with a battle cry which inspired the flagging spirits of his men.

With renewed vigour, they set about slaying their enemies until the horses were wading knee-deep in bodies of moorogs. All the while the Nine Keepers of Avalon stood in the field of battle, waiting until the time was right for them to claim their chosen prizes.

Guinevere's eyes were fixed on the imposing figure of Morgana Le Fay still standing triumphantly on the skyline in the company of a solitary raven. Then Guinevere saw the morning light darken behind Morgana as a cloud of birds flew in from the east. Something caused her to look up, and there, so high she could hardly see them, was a group of hawks hovering on the wing and ready to plummet on prey unaware of their presence.

All the children followed Guinevere's gaze, and as they did so, the hawks dived. There must have been at least fifty of them, and the children ran with Guinevere for the cover of the nearest thing to safety they could find: a small arch in what had once been the south transept of the abbey. By now the birds were clearly visible, and to Jo's horror in particular, they saw the leading bird was a buzzard with red plumage round its neck.

Olric!

The buzzards slowed before landing. They did not seem to be seeking prey after all, because they came down more like pigeons than hawks and stood for a moment in the centre of the abbey's nave. The nine Keepers formed a circle round the birds and began to perform an eerie dance while the knights returned from their rout of the first wave of moorogs.

Guinevere tensed, and the children could not believe their eyes as the buzzards grew in size and shed their feathers. Where there had been wings, now there were arms, and the shapes of birds became those of warriors. Rhiannon stepped into the centre of the circle to touch Olric's red plumage, and she stepped back triumphantly as a fearless warrior was reborn with flame-red hair to match that of his mother.

Mordred had returned in body under the proud eye of his mother, still surveying the battle from her vantage point on the tor.

"Mordred!" whispered Guinevere, stepping back in horror as the impact of this transformation began to dawn on the children.

"This is a nightmare," said James shakily. "I can't believe what I'm seeing. You knew Olric must really have been Mordred, didn't you?"

"I feared as much, yes. When you described the buzzard with the red plumage, it was too much to be a coincidence. Mordred's spirit was released by the goddess and has been locked inside the body of a bird until this moment."

"What about the other buzzards?" asked Jake.

"They are other men who fought and died alongside Mordred at the Battle of Camlann. They too have taken the shape of buzzards until this moment." Lola stared in disbelief, while Jo shivered in memory of the sharp talons gripping her in Smugglers' Cove and the aggressive way Olric had pursued Jake across the field at Penmarrett. James also recalled the moment he'd been pinned to the ground while clinging to Excalibur. All their efforts had been in vain. Hope of survival against such overwhelming odds had been reduced to nil by the arrival of Mordred and his men, especially because Merlin's magical powers were no longer the equal of their enemies.

King Arthur was leading his army back when he saw Mordred facing him at the head of his fighting force, an evil leer across his face as he spoke. "So your Majesty," he shouted scornfully, "you have come back to face death at the end of my sword for a second time!"

"Did you not also fall at Camlann, Mordred? Besides, this time no trickery has stolen my sword from me!"

"Not yet, your Majesty." Again the words were laced with scorn, and Mordred's followers cheered their leader. That cheer soon echoed around the plain by Morgana's army, and it was accompanied by the renewed howling of the Hunter's hounds of war.

The children had forgotten about the dogs, and they looked round to see the wall of flames was beginning to die down. The bared fangs and scarlet eyes appeared more terrifying than ever, and the Hunter himself was already stepping through the embers to stand concealed in the shadows.

"Come on!" urged James, and he leapt out from the arch, followed by the other three children. He removed his shirt and shouted to Jake to do the same. "We can use our swords. Jo, take my shirt and try to fan the flames back to life. Lola, you do the same with Jake's T-shirt. Jake and I will guard you!"

The girls desperately waved the shirts, and sure enough, the embers began to spark back to life, keeping the howling hounds at bay while the boys stood with their swords poised, ready for any dog daring to leap over the fire.

The stag head of the Hunter turned to face them, and the creature raised his spear towards the unsuspecting figures of James and Jake, whose eyes were focused only on the dogs. With a mighty swing, he knocked both boys to the ground, their swords tumbling down to lie beside them. Then he turned his attention to the girls and beckoned them to join the figures lying unconscious on the earth.

Meanwhile, the Keepers settled on the highest walls of the abbey and watched as two lines of warriors marched towards one another. King Arthur and his knights had dismounted in response to Mordred's taunts about being able to fight on equal terms. *It is a strange sort of equality,* thought the watching Merlin, *when one army is surrounded by an overwhelming number of enemies.* He looked into the sky for any sign of hope, but after looking around him, he saw only great numbers of hostile birds occupying the air. It was too late for any salvation.

The yells of fighting men filled the air, and then there was the added din of metal striking metal. All around the abbey walls, there were men

OLRIC!

trying to outwit each other, wielding their mighty swords, and knowing one small error of judgement was likely to spell death.

The battle raged throughout the morning as more and more of Morgana's allies surrounded the men locked in combat, cheering at each blow dealt by one of Mordred's warriors. Guinevere and Merlin were isolated under the arch and were watching helplessly when a new threat appeared behind them.

When the flames flickered and slowly died, the Hunter called his hounds, which leapt over the dying embers. There was the fearsome sound of baying animals lusting after the blood of their enemies. Lola and Jo lay as flat as they possibly could, hoping they wouldn't be noticed, or else they would be ripped apart in seconds by the crazed beasts.

After a while, the sound seemed to have moved farther away, and the two girls cautiously raised their heads. Their relief at being spared a gruesome end was instantly overtaken by despair because they could see the Hunter and his pack surrounding King Arthur and his entire fighting force. The men were still battling bravely, but they were weary, whereas their enemies had fresh swordsmen to take the place of their tiring comrades. Jo looked down to see both her brothers were regaining consciousness.

"My head!" wailed Jake.

"What happened?" groaned James, stooping to pick up his sword.

"You were both clobbered by the Hunter," explained Lola.

"Just be grateful it wasn't the point of his spear," said Jo. "In fact, you can be thankful his dogs didn't fancy eating you."

"I notice they didn't like the smell of you either!" added Jake, now regaining his spirits.

"Of course they didn't. I smell much too nice—not like you!" Jake was about to answer back, but Lola called interrupted.

"Oh, no! Look!" All of them looked up, following her wide-eyed gaze. "They've got Merlin!"

"And Guinevere!" added Jo. "Whatever can we do now?"

They watched dismally as the once proud wizard was marched beside his queen to witness the inevitable end. Suddenly a figure broke out from

The Battle of Avalon Vale

the encircled ranks and ran towards Merlin, Guinevere, and their captors. It was Sir Percival, his sword drawn, and he was charging to their rescue, closely followed by the loyal figure of Cabhan. The enraged knight felled one of the escorts and was starting to fight another when he was stabbed in the back. He sank to his knees, his brave body badly wounded as he gazed at those he had tried to save. Guinevere grasped his hand. While the brave knight lay dying, others came to see off the remaining guards.

Cabhan was fending off four Moorogs close by, and he fell defenceless with his sword knocked from his grasp. The moorogs were poised for the kill, but James rose and charged across the plain, with the other children shrieking in pursuit. In surprise, the creatures turned, and the first one fell with James's sword buried in its chest while Jake engaged in battle with the second. Meanwhile, Cabhan had got back to his feet and was gaining the upper hand against the third. He shouted his thanks for the rescue.

"It is a well-made sword!" answered James, parrying a blow from the axe of his rival while the two girls successfully attracted the attention of the fourth moorog. It was only a matter of time, however, before they were all encircled by reinforcements screeching in triumph. Into their midst strode Morgana Le Fay, her eyes flashing and her mouth curled in cruel satisfaction.

"Take them to join the others!" she commanded, and the despondent frightened children were led back to where King Arthur and a few of his bravest followers were still defying the odds. The blade of Excalibur continued to flash in the midday sun.

The children were led past the snarling dogs and through the ranks of enemy men and moorogs. They found themselves amongst wounded knights. Inside the ring stood the nine Keepers.

"They are waiting for the dead so they can claim their souls in the underworld," said Merlin bitterly. The raven flew down from the tor to stand behind the valiant king, who was ready to fight Mordred, although his strength seemed to be deserting him.

The raven began to transform like the buzzards had earlier. Its feathers became a long black gown which was wrapped round the figure of a woman. Her hair was white as snow, and her face, when she turned to face the captives, was a terrifying blend of wrinkles and green flesh.

OLRIC!

"Annwn!" gasped Merlin. "Goddess of Avalon, Dark Mother of the Dead! She is waiting to take back the great king. The Keepers and the Hunter are here to gather up all who fall on this cursed day."

Morgana smiled at Merlin's reaction. She had waited a long time to score such a victory over him, and there would be no way back for him now.

Neither would there be any triumphant return for King Arthur. Her plans to dominate the world were succeeding in spite of the interference of those children. She allowed herself the luxury of a glance in their direction, where they were standing and looking back at her. She could not believe their defiance until she realised they were not looking at her at all. Their astonished eyes were directed past her shoulders, and she turned before her evil heart missed a beat.

Approaching from the west was a cloud of beating wings, and even from a distance, she could hear the sound of swans in flight. There was only one power on Earth to rival the dark magic of Avalon, and the swans were bearing her from the depths of her own underworld to command Annwn and her Keepers to go back under the marshes.

The children were cheering now as the figures of Aerhwana and her damsels could be recognised sweeping below the clouds. The Lady of the Lake, her white robes flowing out behind her, stood on the leading swan, making an impressive and welcome sight for the beleaguered ranks below.

Annwn returned to the guise of a raven and flew up over the tor, followed by the ghostly figures of the Keepers, which melted back along secret paths into the heart of Avalon. The Hunter stole away with his dogs into the marshes, leaving only moorogs and men to the mercy of the Lady.

The swans swooped low to the cheers of the knights and children, putting the enemy to flight and ruthlessly hacking them down as they fled. Only Mordred stayed with his mother, and the two of them stood defiantly facing the Lady when she returned to stand between Merlin and King Arthur in readiness to receive their surrender.

At that moment, another sound was heard. This time it came from high above, a high-pitched whine preceding a deeper roar, and Morgana yelled happily at this new twist in fortune. Her comet was descending, and she screamed out the words with which she had baffled the nation's government.

> "When Morgana's Comet lights the sky,
> All of Britain rests.
> The future king will surely die
> 'midst explosions in the West."

She cackled, allowing the amended wording to sink in before she continued. "It is earlier than I had planned, but it is well timed under these circumstances. Come, Mordred. Let us leave these people to swim in their own blood." Upon saying this, she swiftly led Mordred away while all the others gazed upwards.

"Merlin." It was the Lady who spoke. "We can prevent this. Show me where the Chalice is etched in the stone. Children, come with us."

"Your Majesty!" called Merlin, his energy restored. "Summon the Round Table to stand around the pillar!"

Merlin stood, touching the carved image of the Holy Grail. Beside him were the Lady of the Lake, the children, Cabhan, and Queen Guinevere. The damsels stood in a group, and the Knights of the Round Table formed an outer circle around them. King Arthur stood amongst them, and all faced outwards with their swords drawn.

The noise was deafening now as the meteor became visible, burning through the atmosphere under Egbert Head's precise guidance. The Lady closed her eyes, and the image of the Grail appeared to lift from the pillar in a blaze of bright light to hover above them. Merlin broke the moment by speaking out, addressing the rock as it screeched down towards the centre of the abbey. The children screamed too, although their voices could not be heard above the din.

"In the name of light, this holy Chalice renounces the evil spirit which controls you!" shouted the wizard. "Pass on from these shores and seek only those who command you!"

The sound continued to increase into an ear-splitting roar. The circle of knights held firm. The image of the Chalice returned to its carving on the pillar, and the meteor swerved away from Avalon, heading a little north of west in search of its creator. After a few moments, it landed with a massive explosion far out in the Bristol Channel.

James looked at the Lady and then at the carving before addressing Merlin. "Is that the …?"

OLRIC!

"Yes, James," replied Merlin. "I did not see it myself at first. The image is very similar to the bell, is it not?"

"Yes, only it's upside down."

"James," said the Lady, "the bell you found amongst the rocks was not the Holy Grail itself, but its outer shape is exactly the same. I forged both of them, yet they both left me for a time."

"When we discovered the carving, I hoped the message I inscribed on it could be heard in Dozmary Pool, and Nimue would come in answer to the call," said Merlin.

"And so she did!" added King Arthur.

"Wow!" said Jake. "Unreal!"

"One and all!" said James, embracing his brother, sister and Lola.

"One and all!" they echoed proudly.

Epilogue

Soon after the comet disappeared over the horizon, the Lady of the Lake gathered the children so they could be carried back to where their parents would expect to find them. Before being settled on the swans, they went to say goodbye to the people from the past who had grown to mean so much to them. Merlin, accompanied by Cabhan, guided them round all the Knights of the Round Table, who were soon to bury the dead. They all assembled together with their king and queen to see the flock of swans take off, and as they did so, the abbey walls echoed with new words to their marching song.

> "We ride at Arthur's side,
> Knights of true honour bound.
> We blaze the trail of the Holy Grail,
> And glory shines around.
>
> 'Tis the fairest age of time,
> When knights patrol the land.
> Against all ill and evil will
> We make our righteous stand.
>
> And the day has surely dawned:
> King Arthur's Court has seen
> Foes put to flight and men to right,
> And a new world will be free."

The swans moved fast and gracefully to leave Lola and Jo at the hotel where their parents and guards were still under the spell of Morgana Le

Fay. The Lady of the Lake lifted the spell as the two girls went back to their room, and the flock departed into the evening sun, heading back to Polzeath.

"Will the knights all go back to Lyonesse?" James asked the Lady as they looked down over Exmoor.

"Yes, and King Arthur and his queen will go with them," she replied. "There, they will await a future calling to restore the fairest age of time."

"And you will go back into the lake, I suppose?" asked Jake.

"Yes. There is always work to be done in the land beneath the waters."

They flew on, mostly in silence, until the Cornish coastline came into view and they could see the red sun begin to sink over the western horizon. As the swans landed in the field where Jake had been chased by Olric, Hilda watched them from the farmyard before coming over to greet them.

"Welcome back," she said warmly, and it was the first time the boys had seen her smile. "We have much to discuss."

Before the boys could reply, there was a loud beating of wings, and they looked round to see the swans fly out over Pentire Point before returning to pass overhead as if in salute. Aerhwana and all the damsels were waving, and the last sight they had of the Lady herself was the white robe flowing behind her as the flock became smaller and smaller in the distance over the moor.

"You saved our sister, didn't you, Hilda?" said Jake.

"I am so glad she is safe, and the other girl too. Whatever price Madame was willing to pay, I could not carry out her orders. It is a pity the men did not see it that way too. McCulloch, Loveless and Growles were not always bad men."

"That's hard to imagine," said James.

"Leatherjacketman and friends can't ever have been good," added Jake.

"Come on. We should go inside," continued Hilda. "You must be hungry, and you ought to have some sleep. Your sister and her new friend are coming back tomorrow. Your mother and father too."

A week later, when the Briscoes had just set off back to London, Matty Petherick went for an evening stroll with his dogs along the shore. Everything seemed so peaceful. The large amounts of magpies and crows seemed to have gone back inland, and the seagulls were less noisy than they had been earlier in the summer. A piece of driftwood caught his eye, and he stooped to pick it up. It was a strip of wreckage from a boat and on it was printed a name: *La Mirabelle.*

Matty looked up thoughtfully, and a pair of cormorants caught his eye. The birds were standing on a rock out amongst the breakers, and if he had been closer, he might have noticed that each had an unusual ring of red feathers around the neck.

Afterword

In the fifth and sixth centuries AD, Britain was far from a peaceful country. The Britons were fighting not only the invading Saxons but the Picts and Scots as well. A new religion, Christianity, was challenging the ancient beliefs, and there was need for the Britons to come together under one banner in order to establish a united realm. These were known as the Dark Ages because there is very little record about what actually occurred in those times. However, the story of one man has stood the test of time as the heroic military commander and devout Christian leader: King Arthur.

Arthurian legends crop up all over the United Kingdom, but many people identify the West Country as the true area where the king grew up and gathered his Round Table at Camelot. This may have been at the site of Cadbury Castle in southern Somerset, but it plays no direct part in the tale of *Olric*. The coastal and moorland areas around Tintagel, however, certainly do. It is not hard to imagine Tintagel Castle overlooking the Atlantic—even in ruins today—as the birthplace of King Arthur and a place where Celts and early Christians might have travelled from Ireland and West Wales. Only five miles away is Slaughter Bridge, which may have been the site of the Battle of Camlann. It is said that Arthur was mortally wounded here and that his sword, Excalibur, was returned to the Lady of the Lake in Dozmary Pool by Sir Bedivere.

Glastonbury lays claim to being the site of Avalon, where Arthur's body may have been brought for burial. Pagan and Christian stories become intertwined with folklore at Glastonbury and its famous tor. Maybe William Blake's "Jerusalem" was inspired by a tale that Jesus accompanied his uncle, Joseph of Arimethea, there: "And did those feet in ancient time walk upon England's pastures green?" The same Joseph is associated with planting the Glastonbury Thorn, which flowers on Christmas Day, and with bringing the Holy Grail to the gates of the underworld at the tor. It is this underworld which is governed by Annwn with the support of her Nine Keepers, and Avalon is sometimes referred to as the Island of the Dead. The tor would have been an island long ago because it rises from land which now lies a little above sea level all the way to the Bristol Channel.

The signs of the zodiac have been read in the contours marking the landscape surrounding the tor, adding to the mysteries of this enchanted place. Therefore it seems appropriate that Merlin should call on astrology in summoning King Arthur and his companions to return from the dead.

Cornwall is rich in folklore, history, and legend. The north coast also provides a blend of beauty and beast, a place to enjoy and inspire but also to respect. There are many dangers for sailors, fishermen, and holidaymakers alike. Although I have tried to keep the story accurately located on the coastline, I have had to take a few liberties with exact places. There is no Trewinnick Cove for example, although there are such secluded beaches along the shore in Port Isaac Bay. At the eastern end of the bay, Tintagel is about ten miles from Polzeath, but for the purposes of this story, it needs to be closer. The lost city kingdom of Atlantis is reputed to lie close to the Isles of Scilly, but for this tale at least, it is better placed north-west of Tintagel.

Standing on the thrift-covered clifftop on the Rumps, with Pentire on the left and the long sweep of the bay out towards Tintagel on the right, it is easy to imagine traders and explorers sailing in from the misty horizon—and to wonder what lies beneath the rolling sea.